MORNING DARK

ALSO BY DANIEL BUCKMAN

The Names of Rivers

Water in Darkness

DANIEL BUCKMAN

MORNING DARK

ST. MARTIN'S PRESS NEW YORK

www.stmartins.com

Book design by Nick Wunder

Library of Congress Cataloging-in-Publication Data

Buckman, Daniel.
Morning dark / Daniel Buckman.—1st ed.
p. cm.
ISBN 0-312-31462-0
1. World War, 1939–1945—Veterans—Fiction. 2. Vietnamese Conflict, 1961–1975—Veterans—Fiction. 3. Conflict of generations—Fiction. 4. Marginality, Social—Fiction. 5. Fathers and sons—Fiction. 6. Grandfathers—Fiction. 7. Illinois—Fiction. 8. Soldiers—Fiction. I. Title.

PS3602.U355M67 2003
813'.6—dc21

2003047151

First Edition: October 2003

10 9 8 7 6 5 4 3 2 1

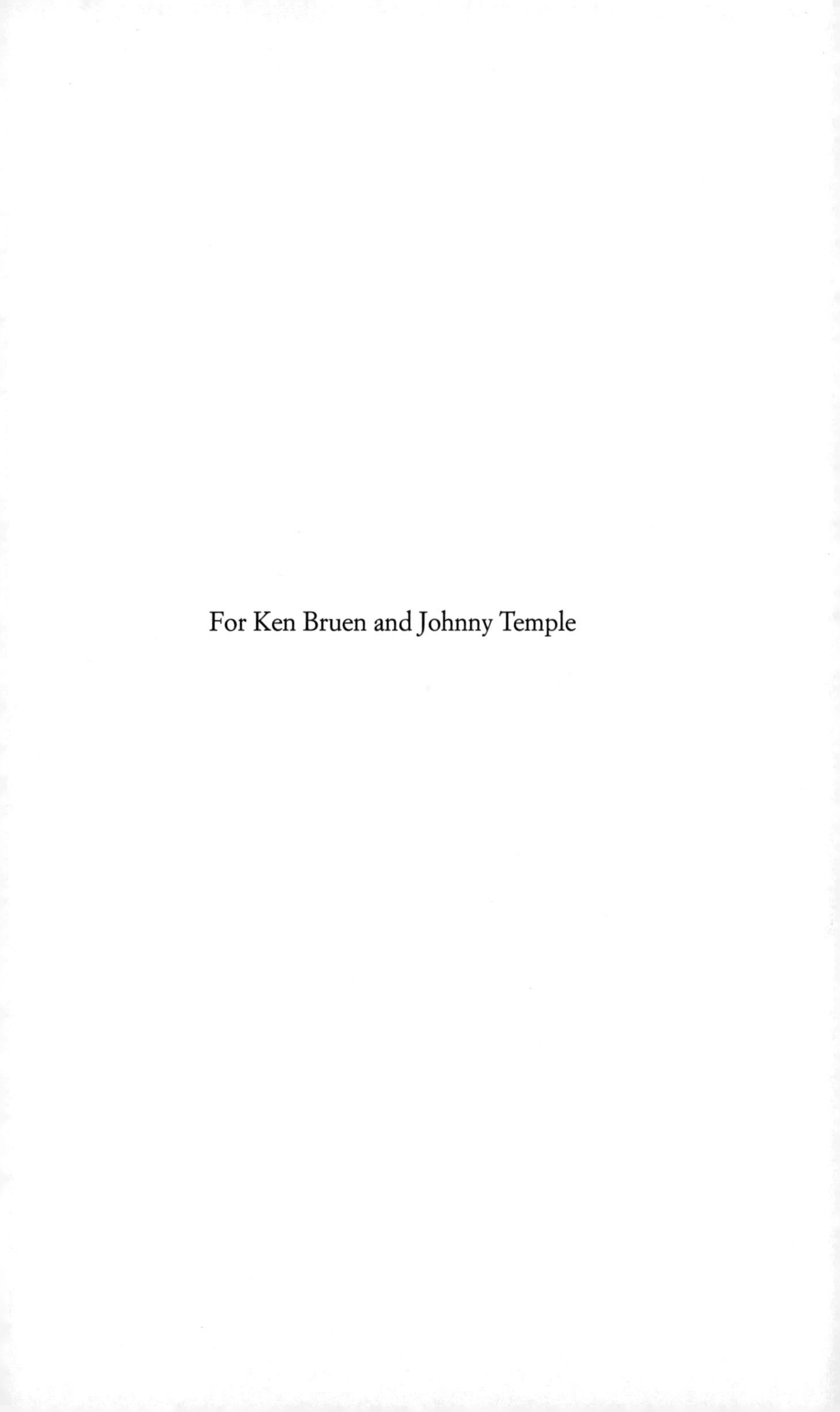

For Ken Bruen and Johnny Temple

ACKNOWLEDGMENTS

The author wishes to acknowledge his debt of gratitude to Rebecca Staton, Johanna Ingalls, and Benjamin Sevier, his editor.

We have forced the Americans to eat soup with forks.

—*General Vo Nguyen Giap*

1

When the old man shot the dog, Walt was not more than five and the November rains bore into the cut fields and the mud jumped as if exploding. The sky sank low and dark and Watega River flooded from the rain and rose back into the bare trees. The morning was fifty years ago, and every autumn Walt swore the rain fell black and filled the furrow lines with murky water, even if his father told him it did not.

The big color always wins and stains the rest, he said, holding the dog by the collar while it howled and snapped air, then put the barrel of the .45 to its head and pulled the trigger, the bullet passing straight through and nicking a hickory root. The dog sagged at the neck and his father kicked the heap into a hole he'd dug that morning before the clouds hooded the country. You better know what to do about things that are too useless for life, he said, looking at Walt and the teeth marks that would scar his cheek. Walt knew the rain was dark, because it turned the silver maples black and darkened the mud between the slanting weeds and made the railroad ties on the berm above the field look charred by fire. He told his father he was wrong. The old man shook his head and took up the shovel from the dirt pile. The rain's clear and the sky's black, he said. Only an idiot worries about this shit longer than a second.

It was not November and the night sank hot and windless. He drove his pickup along 113 and watched the swollen river between the roadside trees, and the dark country smelled green like cornstalks and oak leaves if he forgot the truck exhaust. The sky looked the way it did when he knew November was coming with the black rain, the cloud cover seamless and smeared perfectly between the long horizons where hedgerows stood darker than the night. He left the windows open and drove fast ahead of the gathering storm and held down the bag of pictures on the bench seat. They were a hundred prints of Vietnam. He'd taken them with a camera he'd bought three months ago at Walgreens, the day his nephew Tommy came home from the army with bad paper after eleven years. "I'm taking you back and paying for everything," Tommy'd told him. "All you got to do is live without a cigarette for the sixteen-hour flight. I want you to have a good goddamned time in a place where you saw people blowed away." Walt had gotten wet-eyed and told Tommy he loved him like a son. He'd kept quiet about how the black rain haunted him more than Vietnam ever did.

The overcast was leaden when the old man drove them out of the quarry woods, scowling the way he did after he'd spent all morning in a tree stand and there were no deer to shoot. Walt's son, Teddy, sat between them and took sips off the old man's coffee. He was a ten-year-old boy who got confused telling time, and spelled words the way they sounded. He had brown eyes that never blinked, soft but alert. The old man patted the boy's small thigh and then pointed at Walt. He rolled his blue eyes before he talked.

I told him you can't get drunk and chase whores the night before a hunt, he said. The deer will smell the foulness like hot garbage. Next time we'll leave him to his whores.

Teddy's ears were bright red from the cold. He smiled at the old man for letting him finish his coffee.

Walt let his father have this. He was too hungover for a fight. He'd been out with Ricky Dugan and Gene Tufty at the Web on Sherman Street. Three crying fuckups ten years home from Vietnam and out partying without a thing to celebrate. The Web was full of them, all lined along the bar, admitting they were alcoholics but saying they sure liked the taste. They blamed everything on Vietnam because they could. Nobody called them out except World War II veterans like the old man. He'd gotten the Medal of Honor after jumping into Normandy with the Eighty-second Airborne and taking out two German .88's with rifle grenades. They drank at the VFW across the street and wouldn't have any of it.

The sky turned black when the old man drove from the woods and hit the gravel road. The rain fell in heavy drops. He was done riding Walt and spat tobacco out the window and wiped the juice from his lips with his Carhartt sleeve. Teddy watched the rain turn the trees black. The old man was sad in the way he got when he looked at the boy after he ran the bases backward in a softball game and smiled like he'd done something. Walt dry-heaved and leaned his cheek against the cold window.

Teddy grabbed the old man's veiny wrist and pointed at the thicket. It ran from the bar ditch back to the woods. He was alive like a dog. The old man stopped the truck. Two deer stood in the rain, a ten-point buck and a spiker. The old man looked at Walt with his teeth clenched.

You going to load that weapon and hunt some deer with your boy? he said.

Walt looked at the old man and his brown-stained teeth. His blue eyes begged Walt to belt him. Teddy was already climbing over Walt and opening the door, so Walt followed, loading the double-barreled shotgun on his way out. Sandwich bags full of bread crusts blew from the truck into the wet weeds. Most days, Walt stopped remembering here. He pretended that he'd been standing in the open door for twenty years, watching the bags scuttle across the gravel.

The rain dripped off Teddy's gun barrel. He'd left his orange hunting hat in the truck and the rain straightened the curl in his hair. They ran through the dead leaves after the deer. Teddy stopped in the ditch water past his thighs and shouldered the shotgun. He aimed with both eyes, the way the old man had taught him, but the deer wheeled and reared and leapt a fallen hackberry. The spiker lost his footing in the mud and reeled wildly before balancing and charging into the thicket behind the buck.

Teddy lowered his weapon and blew cold before splashing out of the ditch water. His eyes tremored. He ran off into the pines like a dog not sure of where the scent was leading him. Walt lagged behind and puked twice into the mud. He forgot Teddy couldn't write his own name and followed him as if he were the old man. They separated and swept through the pines in two half circles and kept the tracks between them and drove the deer into the thicket.

Walt saw the buck's rack brushing the low-hanging branches. He even saw his breath rising into the mist like smoke off a cigarette. He wanted to get this done and go home and get drunk all over again while the cold rain iced the windows. He shouldered the shotgun and squeezed the trigger and the buck fell in a heap. He thumbed the safety and moved to the kill. The old man's truck shut down and Walt heard him cussing his way through the thicket.

Walt came to the pine tree and saw Teddy head-shot and dead without even looking. His forehead was tore open and the rain dripped with the blood along his cheeks. Walt went cold. He never wanted to see anything again. He put the barrel in his mouth and pulled the trigger, but the safety was locked. The old man was looking down at him when he looked up. The wad of Levi Garrett bulged from his cheek.

Go on, you son of a bitch, he said. Go right the hell on.

Walt stood grinning and jet-lagged in the doorway of Jarhead's. The rain blew inside and wetted the dirty floor tiles and floated a cigarette butt. He took the Vietnam trip pictures from under his T-shirt. Out in the street, the rain beat against the car windows in tiny squalls and boiled the gutter puddles, the reflected streetlight reeled and broke, and the rain slashed through the foundry smoke twisting from the chimney across the river.

"Back in the world," he said.

Red Ruell wiped the beer spill and cigarette ash off the bar and pushed the peanut shells into the bowl with his hand. The USMC globe and anchor was mottled on his bicep. His snarled hair was gray. Walt closed the door, stomped the rain from his boots, and waited for the bar to dry before setting down the pictures. Larry Anderson dragged on his Winston and leaned on an elbow to see. The ash fell where Red had cleaned, and Walt looked into his bloodshot eyes.

"You got any ears?" Larry said.

"Put it out," he said.

"I just lit the son of a bitch."

"You want to see them?"

"Did any of them old gooks fuck with you?"

Larry took the cigarette from his mouth. His thumb was swollen from a roofing hammer, the nail flat black. He and Red were Khe Sanh marines and had stood the whole siege, the days when a thousand artillery rounds fell from the hills, and the rockets that came when the dinks tired of humping more shells up the wooded slopes. They talked like the whole thing had happened yesterday. "Hell sucks," they said to each other. "Shit happens, jarhead."

"I'll keep it over here," Larry said.

"Pinch it off."

"I'll see the pictures later."

"I ain't explaining them twice."

"I've seen Vietnam before."

"You won't recognize shit," Walt said.

"I'd know them firebases. I was a grunt. You was just an engineer."

"It was the same Vietnam."

"Bullshit. You was a rider. I was a humper."

Larry turned and watched the rain drive against the neon-lit window. Red held the bar rag and whipped it against his hand. Walt set down the picture, a strip of rutted red dirt with coffee trees growing in the background and the sunlight a burning white.

"You ever thought you'd see that red shit again?" Walt said.

"Jesus Christ," said Red.

"You know what this is?"

Larry snuffed the cigarette and the smoke drifted from his mouth. He and Red studied the print and moved their lips silently. Gio Linh. Con Thien. Maybe it was Camp Carroll. Larry lifted his head and met Walt's eyes in the bar-back mirror. Walt grinned and slapped his back.

"I'll kiss your ass if you can tell me what this is," he said.

"In front of people?"

"Right here on pool league night."

Walt could hear the rain rattling against the metal cisterns. Larry tilted his head and studied the print while Red wiped what he already had cleaned.

"That's a dirt road in Georgia, Walt. I bet you and your nephew went fishing."

"It's Khe Sanh. The airstrip."

"No. I sat seventy-seven days in a bunker by that airstrip. The dust ain't red enough. Me and Red would know because we ate enough of it. Shit, that's where Red got his name—he thinks he's sunburned our first day at Khe Sanh until he shaves and the dust washes off."

"I thought I'd been boiled," Red said.

"The place is just too green," Larry said. "There's so much diesel fuel soaked into the ground that nothing could grow for a hundred years."

Walt jutted his chin across the bar and hit them with another picture. It showed a middle-aged Vietnamese man in a khaki war veteran's uniform. His chest was full of tin medals. He smiled and stood very short beside Walt, with the ruined airstrip behind them. The NVA star glinted from his high-fronted kepi. He looked over the sunglasses he pushed midway down his nose.

"What the hell would Charlie be doing fishing in Georgia?" Walt said.

In the soft white bar light and drifting smoke, they looked down at the print. Larry said "Son of a bitch" twice. Red dropped the bar rag and picked up the remote and hit the mute button, but the TV was already off. He stared at himself in the bar-back mirror.

"God that dink looks old," he said.

Walt shook his head.

"He was a sergeant in the NVA. He runs the vistors' center."

"Jesus," said Red.

"He sees me and Tommy and comes running up and shaking our hands, asking if I'm a Khe Sanh veteran. I tell him no, but my buddies back home lived the whole siege. He says he was a veteran, too. 'I in hills,' he says, laughing like a happy drunk. 'You tell you buddies I in hills.' "

Larry looked at Walt. Then he looked at a picture of the vistors' center, a big stucco building with new air-conditioning units outside. There were shots of an old M60 tank, with the long barrel shadowed on the red ground and young Vietnamese guys filling sandbags to construct a bunker. He looked at Walt again.

"They're turning the place into a dink Gettysburg," he said.

"It's already turned," he said.

"Where are the hard-core gooks?" Larry said.

"Old and talking shit," Walt said.

Larry smiled mean. His dark eyes floated and he held an unlit cigarette.

"They probably can't do much else," he said.

Red and Walt looked into the bar-back mirror at the same time. They saw themselves leaned over the pictures among the ashtrays and beer glasses. Red turned away and tried pocketing his hand with the remote in it. Walt nodded at Red, but Red stared at the floor and let his hand hang.

"Just so they know we kicked their ass," Red said.

"It don't matter," Walt said.

He left the pictures and walked out the door.

The rain and the rain shadows blew through the hooped streetlight and the headlights from passing cars bled slowly in the wet black street. He let the rain clean the tavern smell from his nose, the urine reek if the john door wasn't closed, the men stinking of dog food from the pack lines at General Foods. He hated their booze smell when they got drunk and said "Welcome home, bro" like yesterday the C-130 had left Dong Ha for Da Nang and then the world. He'd spent thirty-three years on a bar stool, smelling their discounted GPC cigarettes while Red Ruell mouthed *semper fi* when a vet opened a long-neck beer, forever listening to the oldies station from Chicago, which he turned down only for Bears games and when Turner Classic Movies ran *Sands of Iwo Jima.* He smelled their pepperoni breath during Friday-night happy hour, when Red brought the lingerie models down from Joliet and middle-aged men played barracks grab-ass and talked about a war that back then they couldn't wait to leave. He hated the smell of Red's tobacco juice and how he spat it in a beer can and told you what rank he'd hold if he'd stayed in the marines. "Sergeant major by now, Walt. Probably at the brigade level. I'd of done the full thirty." Sometimes he held his nose against the smells and wished the air would catch fire and consume him first.

He staggered through the rain to his pickup. The truck was left over from the old man's contracting business. Fifteen plumbers became him driving around Watega with a cell phone, waiting to unclog toilets. He drove down Grant Street past the high school and raised his middle finger and the rain danced on the hood.

It was ten o'clock when he got home, and he cut the headlights and pulled into the space between the garages and drank an airplane bottle of Jack Daniel's. He was getting drunk enough to screw his fourth wife, because Patty was a heap naked. He saw sandbags when he looked at her. She squeezed her butt into Wal-Mart blue jeans and went to the great spaces on generic Xanex after splitting a pork lover's pizza with her son Peter, an obese kid who ruined the furniture. He shot back another airplane bottle and opened the door into the rain.

The computer light was splayed blue and yellow against the wet bedroom window. Patty sat up nights chain-e-mailing inspirational writings that had been chain-e-mailed to her. Some had music, flying angels, flowing rivers with water sounds. She e-mailed people so often, they asked her to stop. She filled in boxes with pieces about the importance of family and checked the log to see if they'd read the messages and then cursed when the e-mails were deleted without being opened. The computer pissed Walt off. He'd married her for company, figuring she'd stare at the television while he ranted about the world and used the lines he got off talk radio. She might have hung on every word, but the Internet had ruined that.

He stood in the back door and took off his boots and wiped the rain from his beard. Shep followed him through the kitchen and looked up by his empty food dish, and Walt waved the dog away. He turned on the television and sat down in his wet clothes. The History Channel was rerunning the show about ancient Egypt and spaceships and how the hieroglyphics told you all about the day they'd landed. The sofa arm was loose from Peter's lying back flat and pushing against it with his feet. "The kid's sixteen and he watches *The Brady Bunch* with focus," he'd told Tommy. "He bent the refrigerator door from hanging off it while he stares inside. He's like fucking dick warts."

The steps creaked when Patty came downstairs. Her shadow moved along the wall and he looked away. He dragged on his cigarette deeply and held his breath and looked over at her upturned nose. She was talking to herself. The smoke hung and she fanned the darkness with a handful of papers.

When he looked away, they were sailing, and some landed on the coffee table. She'd found a Web site advertising Asian brides, girls from Thailand and Malaysia, after Walt told her about his R and R in Bangkok thirty-three years ago and how he and Hill had rented girls for the week and bought them new shoes. "They were little things," he'd said. "Kittens. Orchids in a vase."

"Your nephew really had to throw this up in my face," she said.

Walt glanced down at the pages and smoked. They were pictures of thin Asian girls printed off the Internet. He said nothing. Sometimes Patty wanted him in the shower, and the water running down her skin reminded him of sweat.

"I couldn't get them bitches out of my mind," she said.

"Did you breathe the way the doctor told you?" he said.

"I see you fucking them."

Her hands clenched into fists. She was shaking. Sweat beaded under her eyes and slid down her ruddy cheeks.

"Did you and Tommy use separate rooms to?"

Walt tried looking around her at the television. He liked commercials about miracle tools. Wrenches that never marred the bolt head. Shop vacs so powerful, they took up broken concrete.

"Weren't their mouths too small?"

"You've got to get off this," he said.

"I'm just glad my name's on half this house."

Walt laughed and lit another cigarette. He saw the broken blood vessels in her nose, the wrinkles cracking from her eye corners until they disappeared under her dyed hair.

"Take your half now," he said. "I've got the chain saw in the garage."

"I'll make you sell it."

Walt scratched his beard. He'd been this way three times before, buying a house and then losing it, and the woman walked away ten grand richer. The old man wouldn't lend him money for the divorce lawyer again. He got sick to his stomach and his heart palpitated.

"Come here," he said.

"No."

"You know the army kicked Tommy out because he made a soldier kill himself," he said.

"What was he thinking bringing you to Vietnam?" she said.

Walt wished the wind would stop and the rain would fall straight past the window.

2

The old man held the ladder while Tom Jane climbed to the carport roof and sweat from his back. He'd hefted up a plywood sheet to sit on while he painted the corrugated metal. The roof bowed and snapped with his footfalls. The old man's face was deeply pleated and he wore a diaper, and Tom heard the plastic rubbing against his pants when he climbed the ladder rungs. He stopped halfway and lifted up two gallon paint cans.

"Move that board close to the supports," he said.

Tom stood and let the roof give. He held a brush, and the handle was gummy.

"That roof is going to buckle," the old man said. "Get on the wood."

Tom looked around. The carport was between two long apartment buildings, eight units a piece. They were the last ones the old man owned, and he'd once operated forty. The shingles were falling off the barnlike roofs. The cisterns missed nails and hung away. The bicycles of the tenants' children lay in the yellow grass. Tom had spent his youth mowing these lawns and painting the apartments and waiting for the day his grandfather would tell him how he'd won the Medal of Honor the night before D day. He'd been gone to the army for eleven years. He was still waiting for the story.

"You got that about staying on the wood?" the old man said.

"Yessir," Tom said.

"The rivets are rusty. The seams will bust if you stress them."

The old man watched Tom sit on the plywood and open the paint with a screwdriver. He drew his eyes. His face sagged, but the bones were still hard. Tom looked away and brushed the thick black paint along the corrugated seams.

"Paint slower," the old man said. "Long, smooth strokes."

He demonstrated with an imaginary brush. There in the half-light.

"It makes the paint go farther," he said.

Tom did what he was told.

"Slower, goddammit," he said. "Work to do the job, not to get it done."

"This good?" Tom said. He brushed real slow and smooth.

"Make sure you kick the rocks away before you paint over them. The asshole kids throw them up here."

"Yessir."

The old man climbed down the ladder. His diaper made him sweat and it ran down his legs and streaked his blue jeans. He walked without bending his knees and stood in the shadow the ladder left on the broken asphalt. He looked up at Tom and pointed at fresh paint drippings.

"You can't clean a damned thing off asphalt."

Tom glanced down and painted. The white of the old man's diaper showed over his belt. He shrugged, then turned and looked off across the green fields to the west.

"How much you spend taking him to Vietnam?" he said.

"Seven grand for both of us."

"That was all your army money."

"Yeah."

"Walt ever lay down twenty bucks for you?"

"No."

The old man stood and stared out at the cornstalks. He looked back behind himself.

"I gave him a plumbing business. I taught him how to make money. He and his third wife put it up their nose."

Tom painted the corrugated surface. He was broke now, out of the army with a bad discharge.

"You know how my boy gets a woman?" the old man said.

Tom dipped the brush.

"He puts a twenty-dollar bill on a fishing pole and casts it into a trailer park. The first one that comes running gets to go to the courthouse and use my name."

"I thought if he saw Vietnam at peace . . ."

"Barry Baron lost both his legs over there. A mine blew them off in the first week. He runs the biggest Ford dealership in five counties."

The old man propped his paint-smeared boot on a ladder rung. He touched his shirt pocket like he was going after a cigarette, when he hadn't smoked since before Tom was born.

"Patty was too depressed to go to work the whole time you were gone," the old man said. "She sat at the kitchen table, crying to Grandma. I had to hear all about how she wants more sex."

"I was with him for two weeks. He wouldn't shut up about how he needed a pint of Jack Daniel's before the romance."

"I bet he told you getting rid of her would be like getting rid of dick warts."

"How'd you know?"

"I've been listening to him talk shit for fifty-five years."

The old man's face tightened. He kicked a rock across the parking lot. He was a disgusted man.

"I'm going to coffee," he said.

Tom shook his head. That was the old man's code for having to go change his diaper. He hated knowing it.

"Jimmy Ruell's coming by with lunch."

"If you deserve to eat," the old man said.

"I used to make guys paint," Tom said.

"You messed that up."

The old man waved him away with his hand. His bones were still thick, but that was all. He walked off without bending his knees and got into his truck. Tom heard him cursing and slapping the steering wheel. He dropped his keys, Tom thought. Maybe his hands shook too much. Soon the truck started and the old man pulled away and the tires sounded on the asphalt before smacking a pothole. The sunlight blurred across the back window and Tom saw the old man's head jar.

He stood and looked at his long shadow crinkled by the corrugated metal. His lean soldier's body was about a month from going soft. He lit a cigarette and bit it with his teeth. He bent down and fetched a brushful of black Rust-Oleum and let it drip.

Staff Sergeant Tom Jane found Miller dead in the latrine. He took off his drill instructor's hat and came slowly forward. The fat kid slumped on the last stool in a long line of toilets, chin to chest. He'd slit his wrist with a disposable razor and the skin was peeled thinly back. The blood ran in a stream down his hand and pooled against the wall and welled in the glow from the streetlight. Tom breathed and felt weak all the way down. The army was over for him. He looked out the window and waited for Senior Drill Sergeant Sparkman to come back from calling the MPs. The small pine trees that grew along the sand drill field bent backward from the hot wind.

Miller was the weakest recruit in Fourth Platoon. His knees buckled like a dying herd animal on nothing runs. His hands were too small for the monkey bars. Tom Jane called him a fat boy and a prison bitch and even offered him as an example of why euthanasia should be legalized. He made the platoon do push-ups every time Miller collapsed, the hot asphalt blistering their palms. He waited for them to visit Miller in the night with soap knotted into socks, and he thought they did. The humiliation and beatings failed to motivate Private Miller. He only looked at Tom with big cow eyes.

Yesterday, Tom Jane had snapped at him after he marched the new joes to the gas chamber so they could feel the sting of CS. The building was windowless and built of cinder blocks and hidden away in the pine trees. He ordered the platoon to don their protective masks and marched them inside ten at a time. They circled the burning gas and the haze was thick and Tom counted cadence by beating a stick against the wall. Miller's head hung down. He was out of step. Tom fell upon him and tore off his mask and made him breathe the chemical fog until he vomited snot and his fat body caved. Tears wrecked his sight. He forced him to low-crawl across the concrete floor. Fuck it, he'd said. Fuck the goddamned floor. Miller passed out. He went still. The nine joes marched in the circle and kept cadence without Tom's stick tapping the wall.

Sparkman walked into the latrine and stood by the window. He wore freshly starched fatigues and he was an inch away from being a short man. He bit off a chew of Levi Garrett to deal with this and then squatted on his heels and looked at Miller's hacked wrist. The dead fingers dangled and splayed, the palm slick with blood. Sparkman tilted back his drill sergeant's hat and shook his head.

The kid worked hard at it, he said. You find the razor?

I didn't look for it, Tom said.

He must have slashed for a good five minutes. The fucker broke a sweat, Sparkman said.

Sparkman pointed out the sweat rings beneath Miller's armpits. His T-shirt was soaked and it clung to the fat rolls around his waist.

Did you have to pull his gas mask off in front of nine joes?" Sparkman said.

You ordered me to motivate him.

Nine joes didn't see that, Sergeant Jane.

The barracks lights were harsh and white. Outside the latrine, the joes walked around their bunks in stocking feet, too scared to talk. Sparkman stood and wiped his hands even though he'd touched nothing.

The joes will tell the MPs everything you did to Miller, he said. I'm just getting you ready.

Tom Jane breathed, but the weakness was gone. He wanted to kick Miller where he slumped dead. Sparkman fixed his hat brim so it set low over his eyes.

Nien went through this a few years ago, Sparkman said. Some shitbag hung himself. This fat congressman from New York City, guy named Cohen, came down here asking questions. The old man threatened Nien with court-martial and Leavenworth. But they just threw him out for the good of the army. He's managing a Taco Bell someplace in New Jersey.

Sparkman looked at him and nodded a long minute before leaving the latrine. In the barracks across the sand field, the fireguard's flashlight strobed between the windows while he counted the joes sleeping in their bunks. Miller's flashlight lay on the edge of the sink. The weakness was back when Tom Jane breathed.

The next week, he stood by the orderly, waiting to sign out of Delta Company. The morning was white from the heat. Sparkman and Jackson reclined in metal swivel chairs with their drill instructor's hats brim-down on the desks. Jackson was a quiet black from Los Angeles who had played college ball before the army but never mentioned which college or what kind of ball. His two front teeth were gold-capped. He glanced at Tom over the top of his Penthouse *"Letters" and continued reading.*

They all wore the same camouflage fatigues, but the stripes were gone from Tom's collar. The two squares where they'd been sewn were darker than the rest of his uniform. No congressman came to the company area, but the old man busted him and chaptered him out of the army. He'd overstepped the acceptable limits. He was told no more. The old man signed the Article Fifteen with the same grim face that had welcomed him to the Tenth Training Battalion. They're here to learn how to bayonet a Muslim's face, he'd said, and you're here to teach them. He wore the combat patch from the Americal Division, the four white stars encased in blue, Lieutenant Calley's old division. Rumor went that the old man's unit had been close enough to My Lai to hear. In two months, he'd left for the Army War College, guaranteed his full bird and one star. Tom Jane was headed back to Watega, Illinois, and his uncle Walt and what was left of his grandfather's contracting business.

Sparkman turned the pages slowly of the Playboy *opened on the desk. The issue was titled "Girls of the Big Ten." He grinned at Tom and filled his cheek with Levi Garrett.*

The best part about being a drill sergeant is all the fuck books you get for nothing, he said. Every new joe that steps off the bus has three. The recruiters must be telling them infantry school is one big circle jerk.

Jackson turned the page and nodded without looking up. His fatigues were tailored so that nobody could miss his muscles.

But you don't read fuck books anyway, Jane, Sparkman said. I bet you never even dicked a hooker.

No, Tom said.

It's a goddamned freak thing, Sergeant Jackson, Sparkman said.

Shit, Jackson said. Jane volunteered to be a drill sergeant and the army won't even give him bus fare home.

I thought I was going to be a recruiter, Sparkman said.

Recruiters the shit, Jackson said. All them high school girls hanging around your desk.

Sparkman spat tobacco juice in the garbage can and looked into Tom's eyes without losing sight of Jackson. Jackson drank half a Coke with one swig.

I know where Jane can get some good whores before he leaves, Jackson said.

He ought to go to the Blue Marble, Sparkman said. The girls drink whiskey with you.

Them bitches are tattooed and toothless, Jackson said.

It's not the face you're fucking.

The Blue Marble's Cracker heaven. The Stoplight has the best whores in Columbus, Georgia.

All that's out there is Koreans, Sparkman said.

Jackson rolled his eyes.

The best whores are in Germany, he said.

Munich is where you should go, Jane. Every one of them is like a porn star.

The trim's all up in Frankfurt.

You got The Wall in Munich, Sparkman said. There's African girls who are still aboriginal.

They watch the clock at The Wall.

The sweat ran down Tom's back and legs and soaked into the waist of his pants. Sparkman smiled at him. His teeth were yellow.

When you a civilian? he said.

When Captain Anderson gets back from chow and signs my papers, Tom said.

You headed home.

I thought I was home.

That silly asshole Miller pimped you.

Sparkman put the Playboy *in the top desk drawer and looked at his watch. Jackson leaned back in the swivel chair, his eyes closed, feigning sleep. Tom imagined him in post office blues after retirement, banging some mouthy black girl with fake fingernails on the mailbags in the back of the truck. He didn't know if they were jealous or disgusted about his chapter discharge. He guessed they were jealous because, like so many, they were lifers for lack of a better idea.*

The sun was no longer a sphere and the sky above the fields glared wide and white. The clouds were burned away and to the east rose the smokestacks of Chicago Bridge and Iron above the empty railroad siding, and between them the sheets of dust rolled like brown water waves. Tom dabbed up the last paint in the can and thought how he'd pay money for rain smells, the sudden cool on the backside of hot wind, and to lie flat while the drops settled the dust and maybe washed it all off him. He was dreaming himself soaked to his burned skin when the woman came out of the end apartment unit and lay upon her stomach on the lawn lounge, a towel spread over the nylon webbing. She undid the thin bikini strap and the cups slid down enough to show her white breasts. She held a book flat in the yellow grass, a thick paperback from the grocery store, shading her eyes to read. Her legs raised. Her ankles crossed. Tom Jane smelled the coconut oil, and for a moment the dust and the Rust-Oleum had no scent at all.

Yesterday, he'd talked to her after the old man left for more paint. She'd looked over her Ray•Ban's and held her place in the book with a finger. Her eyes were brown like her hair. A beeper and cell phone lay beside the book. She'd let him see the white tops of her breasts.

"I was in the army for eleven years," he'd said. "I jumped out of airplanes. Perfectly working ones."

She'd looked down at her book, then smiled at him again. Winged grasshoppers jumped from the weeds along the side of the field.

"I haven't been out long," he'd said. "But jumping out of airplanes is what I miss the most."

The woman had nodded without smiling.

"You got the day off?" he'd said.

"I'm a resident at Saint Mary's," she'd said.

"I was born there. My name's Tom Jane. I was a staff sergeant, on the list for E-Seven when I got out. I'd probably be that by now. I was a drill instructor last thing. That helps you get promoted faster."

The woman had forced a close-lipped smile and shaken her head, not looking over her glasses anymore.

He'd said good-bye, and she was silent. He'd climbed the ladder and knelt on the plywood sheet, then dipped the brush and painted over the dust, the grit hardening with the Rust-Oleum.

Today, she didn't look at him. He kept to his brush and eyed her and her thin shadow against the dried grass. The wind mounted, small gestures of a breeze, and off in the cornfields blackbirds flew close over the tassels. The hot paint bleared his eyes while he stole glances at her body, dreaming himself a drill sergeant again, his camouflage fatigues starched, his jump boots polished like glass, the campaign hat low over mirrored aviator sunglasses. He made the new joes march, these scrotum-headed peons, bullying them into step with insults from Hollywood movies that got civilians laughing. This woman watched, a yellow dress over her soft curves, her panties and bra visible beneath the linen. He was a man. He was something to see. Master jump wings on his chest, the ranger tab upon his left shoulder. She wanted his uniform off, her hands clamped on his hard body. He sensed that from the way she played with her hair. Later, after the new joes were in their bunks, masturbating to the thought of pregnant girlfriends, he and this woman made love in the pine trees beyond the parade field, near a small creek where water sounded in the rocks, smelling kudzu, the hot Georgia dark. Her breast was in his mouth, her small hand on his penis. She was married but had sneaked away from a husband who was stark and white like a hospital corridor.

He and his father stood in the garage door and waved to his ride home from the Boy Scout's camping trip. He was a tall man who looked thin but was not thin at all. The wind stripped the yellow leaves from the oak trees and the leaves were dry in the sunlight and the wind drove them into the garage. His father kept waving long after Jack Nowack's Bonneville disappeared down the street. Tom dropped his backpack. They watched the leaves blow across the yard, the reds and yellows caught in a whirlwind, and after a minute, his father looked at him vacantly and said his mother had left with Pete Taylor. That was all he told him.

His father walked from the garage. The sunlight strobed the cheek his mother had gored with her fingernails. She'd done this before, after throwing her bourbon and water at him from across the kitchen, calling him a fucking prince, then launching from her stout legs the way a cat starts to fight. She screamed and spat and her fingernails sliced against his face. She left the house with a cigarette in her mouth. He bent down and picked up the ice cubes and the broken glass.

Tom sat on his backpack and imagined telling his mother how glad he was that she'd left. A relief, he'd say. There were no more of her tantrums. The half-drunken swearing. The crazy, mean eyes. That was over and he could finally tell her how much he hated her for them. There were times, he'd tell her, that the hate was like a rain inside him, a heavy freezing rain.

He went in the house when the bird shadows faded from the driveway. His father sat at the kitchen table, surrounded by her small things, the hooped earrings in a clean ashtray, her Salem smoke faint in the carpet. His eyes were spent from crying and he looked strange without his glasses. The dusk was wild and cold-blowing; spinning sticks hit the windows.

I want to get your rifle and shoot them both, Tom said.

His father did not know how to look at him. Tom told him about shooting them through the window where they were doing it. Two shots, two kills. His father stood up and slapped him so that his cheek touched his shoulder. Tom bit his tongue to keep from crying.

That's not the way of our Lord, he said.

Somebody has to get them, Tom said.

His father hit him again. He turned his face into the force of the slap.

I'm not afraid, Tom said.

He watched his father cry. Tom knew his father could teach him nothing about being a man. His father looked at the hand he'd used to hit him and cried harder.

The weeks passed, the short autumn days of bad weather. His mother rented a duplex in East Watega, beyond the railroad crossing at North Street. He burned her pictures in the river woods and buried the ashes beneath a wet rock. She phoned once and said something in a limp voice about loving him unconditionally. He hung up. His sister was small and quiet, with dark eyes. Tom never knew what she thought about any of it. Their father left every morning in his shopkeeper's shirt and tie to sell furniture at his store on Grant Street and then drove home after making the night deposit to fry them hamburgers. He hid from it all in broad daylight.

The dusk was dirty and gray one Saturday night when Pete Taylor and his mother were coming to pick up his sister. He waited upstairs with his father's .30–30, a lever-action Winchester, and drew a bead on the cars passing down the street. He loved snipers in the war movies, the way one man reduced a squad to madness among the ruins of a French town. He imagined winning the Medal of Honor like his grandfather. After school, he drew down on Davy Sorbo and Eddie Olszewski while they shot baskets in Sorbo's netless hoop. He followed Mr. Zasada and his oblong head the length of the driveway when he stepped from his car. He levered back the hammer and held them in his sight, then dry-fired. They were German soldiers he'd been sent to kill. One time, he loaded the rifle and aimed at Davy Sorbo's mom, shapeless in a housedress and kneesocks, and laughed while she opened the mailbox.

The headlights from Pete Taylor's red Camaro hit the garage door. He concealed himself by standing away from the window at an angle. It was not dark enough for the headlights to shine back in their faces. Pete Taylor sat behind the wheel, his eyes jock-cool, like the men in aftershave commercials. His mother wore sunglasses and looked out the window. This woman who had gone from a shopkeeper to an insurance salesman had another move planned. He shouldered the rifle and his sight picture upon their foreheads was lined clean. He shot Pete Taylor before his mother. The hammer fell dry. Tom wanted Pete Taylor's brains covering the window where she looked out, as if searching for the next place to land.

Pete Taylor honked the horn.

My father comes out the front door into the fading twilight, where the wind blows crooked sticks from the trees. Both fists are clenched. He shows teeth and moves across the yard. The wind blows the screen door open. His face is wet from the rain.

Pete Taylor leans back on the seat and honks the horn again. He smiles around his glowing cigarette. His game is other men's wives and tonight he ranks on the board.

My father wears no glasses and stares straight ahead through the rain. He is lethal, like the cold wind before the snow falls, and walks so fast that no shadow streaks across the dead leaves.

He opens the car door and grabs Pete Taylor by the throat and pulls him into the wet wind. Pete screams. His knees go slack. He stumbles while the rain undoes his blow-dried hair. My father smiles, his eyes unblinking, before pushing Pete Taylor into the door well and slamming the door on his head. Paul's arms hang awkwardly behind him. My father slams the door five times, then ten, his movements deliberate as dance steps. Pete Taylor coughs for his breath.

I love my father.

Only his sister came outside with her clothes in a grocery bag. She was small and moved like a cat in the wind. The rain streaked the paper sack. She climbed into the backseat and Pete Taylor reversed down the driveway, the red of the taillights bleeding on the wet cement. Tom held a bead on the car and followed it up the street.

The wind filled the curtains when the light came on in his room. He heard his father start to speak in his slow way, but he said nothing. The curtains touched the ceiling. Tom lowered the rifle and turned.

I could have killed him and her both, he said.

His father loosened his tie and unbuttoned his collar. Tom knew that his father didn't recognize him anymore.

I blew out all my breath before I aimed, he said. The way the old man taught me. I held the sight right on his head.

His father came at him like a sleepwalker. His eyes were red. He took the rifle by the barrel. Tom waited to get hit, but there was only the rain sounds.

I have to do a better job of hiding this, his father said.

He left the room without shaking his head, and Tom looked back out the window. The branches were beating against the house. Out in the street, the rain slashed through the water stand-

ing at the curbs. The wind blew into his eyes and they numbed. He decided to become a professional soldier. He could go in four years. No man ever took from a soldier.

Tom saw the second rock coming before the first one hit the roof. The Rust-Oleum can jumped and the rocks were rimed with field dirt and they marked the new paint. The sun glinted in his eyes. He rose suddenly and saw black spots and felt as if water were taking him over the side. Then Jimmy Ruell's red face appeared above the roof edge and he handed Tom two beer bottles. He held a bag of hamburgers with his teeth and grease stained the brown paper. Tom took the bag and wiped his forehead with his shirtsleeve and it came away wet. He sat down with the beers.

"I thought I was going to have to whip somebody's ass," he said.

"Lifers call the MPs. They don't fight. They just draw up paperwork and flag your personal file."

Jimmy stepped upon the roof with a small bucket of iced beer. The corrugated metal buckled and he grinned and jumped up and down. He sweat everywhere, the way drinkers do.

"Sit your ass on the plywood," Tom said.

They opened the beers with car keys and lit cigarettes.

"You take these from Jarhead's?" Tom said.

"They're hotter than this roof."

"You better stop playing or your old man won't sell you the bar. Red Ruell stayed green, stayed marine."

"You find any of his shit at Khe Sanh? I bet it's petrified by now. Them Vietnamese kids load up their slingshots with it and hunt monkeys."

"You should have come seen for yourself," Tom said.

"I wasn't dropping three grand to see what I can't stand hearing about anymore.

"At least you got some over in the Persian Gulf."

"I saw worse barracks fights at Camp Lejene."

Tom waved him away and dragged on his cigarette.

"I was a marine, but now I'm not," Jimmy said. "I just want to be in business. I got some ideas for the bar. Food, live music, a beer garden for summertime. Gut the whole place."

"Where the old jarheads going to go?"

"The old men will be dead by then. They can go over to the VFW and run the fish fries. I want to make money."

"No more benefit spaghetti dinners for POW/MIA families?"

Jimmy pointed at the sunbathing doctor. She had her bikini bottoms rolled down to tan the flesh there.

"That's my new customer base," he said.

"Forget it, Ruell."

"That girl don't fit in around here."

"She's a resident. A doctor."

"I know what a resident is. She won't be this broke in a few years."

"The old man is always over there fixing something," Tom said.

Jimmy laughed while Tom looked through the beer bottle at the blurry white sky.

"Go run your soldier-boy lines," Jimmy said.

"She wouldn't take her clothes off and jump me for sixty bucks."

"So your lines didn't work?"

"An educated woman can be real polite about telling you to get lost."

"The problem is, you need them," Jimmy said.

"You don't need those kind."

"They make another brand somewhere?"

"Vietnam," Tom said.

"You can think some shit," Jimmy said. "The only difference between you and Walt is four wives and a bar tab."

"You should have seen them in Hue City. They wear these long silk dresses and silk pants. Usually white or yellow. You can just see the outline of their bikini underwear. Every one of them is a perfect B cup. They're so quiet and pretty and they just look at you with these soft brown eyes when you talk and you just know a woman like that ain't going to punish you later for not living up to her daydream. I met one and her name's Tuyen. It means 'stream' in Vietnamese. They name their girls after flowers and rivers and trees like that."

"Was she looking at you with her brown eyes?"

"Yes."

"What's it feel like to be a dollar sign."

"Shut up, Ruell."

"I bet she needs money for school."

Tom flipped his cigarette butt at Jimmy and it bounced off his arm and went off in the wind.

"What did you really see over there?" Jimmy said.

"A bunch of Vietnamese. They smile at you in the hotels and ignore you in the streets."

"He's telling people you ditched him and went whoring."

"I've heard."

"He said he was having panic attacks in the hotel and you were running around Hue with some little thing."

"I got a motor scooter ride."

"I know it."

"He talked the whole trip about how he couldn't stand seeing her come out of the shower. He was going to send her packing when he got back."

"I can see him saying it," Jimmy said. "Drinking his beer real thoughtful. Waving his cigarette like a wand. He came back and got shit-scared of losing her."

Tom looked out at the fields and smoked. The wind whirled dust over the cornstalk tassels and he could see the doctor trying to use her hands against it. She coughed while the dust lined her long hair strands and got under her sunglasses and stuck to her oiled skin. Jimmy finished his beer.

"I hate Vietnam veterans," he said.

"Jesus Christ."

"Red Ruell and Walt Michalski had something to come back to. They just thought they didn't. Their fathers had businesses. Your grandpa was a plumber. Mine was a carpenter. They built half the houses in East Watega."

"So?"

"All they did was run those businesses into the ground, then sit in taverns and talk shit. My old man opened a bar and called it Jarhead's. He still talks in his grunt lingo."

Tom waved Jimmy away with his hand. "Not all of them did that," he said.

"I tend bar. I hear them every day of my life. Most of them wish they could be stuck in the first year they came home."

Tom opened a second beer and looked into the sun. "I really can't say I blame them."

3

Walt closed his toolbox on the kitchen table. Patty smiled and moved closer while he drank back the coffee. He looked out the window above the sink at the rain in the street. She held her robe closed and gave him bedroom eyes borrowed from a soap opera. She wanted to be sexy for him and had made the robe like a kimono, sewing it herself from red satin. It was hard to watch.

"I got a call," he lied. "A septic line out in Wichert."

She let her robe fall open, her breasts so white, he saw the blue veins. He stared at last night's dishes in the drying rack. She ran a finger over his knuckles. He smiled and took his car keys from his pocket, looking back out the window. The rain fell straight through the tree branches and rattled the maple leaves.

"I got to be out there before eight. He said the ground is bubbling around the line."

When he picked up the toolbox, her chubby fingers slid up his arm and over the Marine Corps globe and anchor. She looked down at his fly. The kitchen counter was covered with potato chip bags and packages of generic cookies. Her fake fingernails were up his T-shirt and she scratched hard, giving him the look, her eyes lost in her oily face. The wind came with rain and beat some leaves from the tree. *Son of a bitch.* He sat down on the kitchen chair and unzipped his fly and hoped this was all she wanted.

The gray clouds welded shut the sky when Walt left the house, and the streetlights had not shut off from the night before. He never looked at the screen door to see if she watched after him. He made his usual loop through town, waiting for the cell call to unclog a toilet, taking Grant Street to the truck stop by the interstate exit, then past Liberty Gardens trailer court, and the Motel Six with the Magic Fingers beds. He lit a cigarette. He drove just to drive.

For twenty years, the whole town had looked at Walt like he smelled bad for killing his son. Diner coffee counters went silent when he took a stool to order eggs. Jack Wiscnowsky, one of the old man's plumbers, got so nervous when they worked together in crawl spaces that he sweat on cold days. Nobody hunted with him anymore except the old man. Red Ruell offered to buy his fancy British slug gun with the Leopold scope, since he probably didn't want it anymore. Men wondered how he could live with himself but were too afraid to say the words. Over the years, Walt learned that people asked with their eyes what they could never speak. I'm living fine, he wanted to tell them all. You wake up in the night for a while, but that stops.

The guys at Jarhead's sat at the bar and always wanted to know if he was all right. Larry Anderson got drunk first on Friday nights and came over and sat by Walt where the bar curved into the wall. He patted his back. He wanted to know if Walt was squared away with things. "Marine to marine," he said, "you know. If there's anything you need, Walt." Then Larry hugged him and said, "Welcome home," and soon started in with the Vietnam nostalgia rap. The unit reunions where they sat around drinking in the hospitality suites of hotel airports in Atlanta. Memorial Day motorcycle rides to the Wall in Washington, D.C. "A room full of blood brothers, Walt. They'll help you get through everything." Thirty years ago, they couldn't wait to forget these people, but Walt kept his mouth shut about that. He listened, and told his old stories, even getting wet-eyed with them. Nobody at Jarhead's could speak two sentences without the third being about Vietnam. But talking about the war with another vet was the one time Walt knew the conversation was about itself, and the guy wasn't thinking, *He killed his own son with a shotgun, opened his head right up.*

The old man had given Walt the plumbing business when they'd stopped making dog food in Watega. The stove factories were already gone to Sonora, Mexico. The plant windows were covered by masoned cinder blocks and weeds poked through the cracks in the parking lot. For ten years, the steel mill on Hennepin Road had sat empty, fenced off, with security guards running shifts in a shack. Domino's delivered out there, but not Pizza Hut. Now General Foods was gone and the taverns in East Watega would not smell like dog food when the men off the day and afternoon shifts drank draft beer with hands red from the processing dye. The last man in Watega better not forget to turn off the lights. That was what people were saying when Walt inherited six trucks, ten plumbers, and Ellen Walker, the old man's heavyset dispatcher, who never remarried after her husband got it in the Chosin Reservoir. The Marine Corps sent her his Purple Heart. She displayed the medal at her desk like it was really something. All he did was catch a bullet, the old man always said, but never to her.

Walt let them go one day and sold the building and all the trucks. There was no new construction. A contractor was like a blacksmith in Watega, Illinois. He went into the service business and drove around the streets of bungalows where the old man had made $3 million running pipe and connecting toilets to sewer lines, waving at the old men who lived behind the picture windows, past commanders of the VFW post, retired on fat union pensions and telling their grandsons how lazy they were, and how hard it once was. The old man's business was down to Walt and a cell phone. He waited for calls to unclog toilets from the lonely wives of long-haul truckers, twenty-five-dollar jobs, and sometimes made a full hundred to fix a farmer's septic line. But the old man blamed him for letting the business fail. "You Vietnam veterans would rather cry than work," he said. "You got to get out there and bid the big jobs."

He took it for three years, while the only new construction was Red Lobsters and Old Country Buffets. They came with their own crews, nonunion guys who drove new pickups with out-of-state plates and stayed at the Comfort Inn out by the interstate exit. They drank beer at the bar of Chi-Chi's, buying strawberry margaritas for divorced schoolteachers and running lines on the girls from the community college who served up the chips and salsa a truck delivered every Tuesday and Friday afternoon. They were the money guys in town and they lived two to a hotel room. The old man never got it. "You got to beat bushes," he kept telling Walt. "You got to hunt money like pheasant."

He pulled into the Hardee's parking lot, where fat women

with fat kids lined up in station wagons at the drive-through windows. The last diner on Grant Street had closed two years ago and the old men had to meet at the Hardee's or Burger King, both of which shared a parking lot with Wal-Mart. The terrors of Anzio and Okinawa sat in plastic orange booths and gulped coffee from Styrofoam cups while some kid with bad acne played air guitar behind the cash register.

He walked inside and the lights were brighter than hard sunlight. Jack Turner looked up at him with his gaunt face from the booth by the window. Last year, cancer had taken his left eye and now he wore a patch under his glasses. He'd worked for the old man back in the old days and his hands were calloused from the heavy pipe wrenches. He talked about checking the rucksacks of the dead German soldiers for schnapps during the Battle of the Bulge. Walt waited for the rest of the story, but he never told one. Turner was haunted like that. The old man loved him because he could work alone in the crawl spaces. "He talks to himself down there, but I don't got to check his work."

Walt slid into the booth and took the lid from the Styrofoam cup. Turner wiped salt off the table with the back of his hand. They lit cigarettes and Walt blew the steam off his coffee.

"I always ask them for some ice in the bottom of a cup," Turner said.

"I know you do."

"There's no sense in making coffee that hot."

"Where they at?"

"Pajak just left after making a mess with the salt. Stremkowski went home."

"Why can't he use the can here?" Walt said.

Turner rolled his good eye.

"Strem can go two places—home and Blue's Café, and

Blue's ain't around no more. Your dad never started work until Strem cleared the john at Blue's."

Turner needed more coffee and he looked over his shoulder. A kid with a tattooed neck was sweeping cold french fries off the floor.

"There ain't no waitresses here," Walt said.

He pushed the cup away and waved his hand and looked out the long, rainy windows. They were building an Outback Steakhouse across Route 50, a Friday's next to that. The workers sat in their pickups, out of the hard rain. The trucks had Michigan tags.

"You find any blue-eyed half Polacks in Vietnam?" He said.

Walt lit a cigarette and shook the match cold.

"No."

"You recognize anything?"

"I had the feeling I was there, but the place looked different."

Walt shook his head. Turner was looking out the window, watching the rain hit the out-of-state pickup trucks.

"You can set right here in Watega and feel that way," he said.

"I don't know. In two weeks over there, I felt like I'd aged thirty-three years. I just wish I could come back again the first time. That's what haunted me the most."

"You find the roads you built?"

Walt nodded. In thirty-three years, this was the most an old man had ever asked him about Vietnam.

"That's better than I'd do if I went back to France. I doubt they left the dead Germans in the fields."

"They still use them roads. Pretty much anything worth a shit, we built."

Turner worked a toothpick. It kept him from smoking so much.

"I saw your dad yesterday. You know what the worst part is about seeing him shit his pants?"

Walt said nothing. They watched a teenage girl pick up trays from the top of a garbage can. She stepped on a french fry and it burst like a bug. Turner's eye white went red.

"You wonder how far you are away from it," he said.

"Fuck him," Walt said. "My old man never cut people slack."

"I remember after the war, when the business was big. We had seven crews of plumbers and all our jobs was new construction. Your old man knocked some Chicago Heights wop out cold with a pipe wrench for trying to shake him down. One time, this big German-looking son of a bitch from the plumbers' local came around handing out pamphlets. Your dad chased him off. He looked right at him and said that during the war he'd killed a lot of Krauts who looked just like him, so he'd know how to do it if the SOB ever came back."

"He won't even look at me," Walt said. "Does he talk to you?"

"He bosses Tommy around these days."

"My nephew is hoping to get the last of the money, Jack."

"That ain't true."

"Does my old man talk to you?"

Turner shook his head. The white hair sprouting from his nose was flecked with cigarette ash.

The rain stopped and the sky turned clear and windy. The construction workers got out of their trucks. They were masons, setting concrete blocks for the walls over long bolts, and wore hard-plastic knee pads. Turner looked at Walt's cell phone and his good eye bleared.

"Their companies bring in their own outfits," Walt said. "Plumbing. Electrical. Everything. I couldn't afford the insurance to bid a job like that."

"I guess so."

"There's nothing to guess."

"There just should be a way back."

They smoked another cigarette and stared past each other in the booth for five minutes before Walt said good-bye and walked to his truck. When he pulled away, Turner sat in the wet window, just the lone silhouette of him, staring at the orange plastic.

Walt drove with one hand and reached under the seat and took out his Bronze Star in the leather case. He'd won the medal for unknown reasons after a long, bad night at Con Thien when the gunnery sergeant lost his head at the neck, the stock of his M14 rifle shot away before he could shoulder it. "What is this for?" Walt had asked the lieutenant. "You did your job," he'd said. "You picked your targets and shot them down one by one." Walt had done just that, from the prone, aiming, then breathing out before squeezing the trigger, like the DI'd said: "A finger on the trigger is like a hand down the panties. Gentle, shitbirds. Real soft."

He was one night home from Vietnam before he knew the leather case had a smell. Like nice shoes or new boots. He sat at the kitchen table with the old man, still freaked by the smell of Downy fabric softener his mother used on the sheets, the spray net in her poofed-up hair when she'd kept sticking her head in the room last night and saying, Are you all right, Wally? The old man sat the leather case down beside his blueprint. He squinted through his glasses and measured the sewer line with his finger. He knew exactly how many feet his index finger represented on the blueprints. Walt waited for him to open the case, but he did not. It sat beside the old man's cold coffee, flecked with ashes from his Camel. He pulled loose tobacco off his tongue and then measured the sewer line again with his finger.

It's too damned close to the gas main, he said.

Walt lit a cigarette. His eyes burned from the smoke. He pointed at the case. Look inside, he said.

I've seen a Bronze Star before, the old man said. It won't do your work for you.

Walt snuffed his Camel hard before he'd half-smoked it. The ashes jumped and lay strewn across the old man's blueprint and the old man wiped them off with his hand. His knuckles were gray and the ashes still streaked the blueprint, so he wiped it again.

Medals don't hold shovels, the old man said.

He worked the next day with the old man, digging new sewer lines off Hobbie Avenue, where the blacks lived in shacky wood-frame dwellings. It was a Public Works project and the old man loved bidding government jobs. He made less money, but the government paid and there was never a lost afternoon in small-claims court. Instead of smelling the springtime dirt, Walt couldn't chase the new leather out of his nose. Good shoes and new boots.

The old man called out from the house's crawl space for a pipe wrench and Walt went to the truck in the alley. He opened the cap and pulled it from the tool bin, made from sheet metal by the old man. A small rain started. He turned from the truck when a black came from between the garages with two dogs. It startled him and he dropped the wrench. The black had a young face, but in his hair were curlicues of gray. The dogs had cloudy eyes and strained against the rope he used for a leash. Walt breathed with difficulty.

Give me the truck keys, the black said.

Walt looked at the pipe wrench where it lay on the alley gravel.

I'll let my dogs loose, the black said. I'll be playing fetch with your dick.

The black let some slack from the ropes. The dogs took it quickly and snapped close to Walt's thighs.

The old man came into the alley, cursing Walt for moving too slow. His face was sweaty and dirty from the crawl space. The rain hit his face. When he saw everything, he started laughing. Walt knew he kept a snub-nosed .38 hidden away in his tool belt. The black didn't know if he should watch the old man's eyes or his hands. The dogs backed Walt against the bumper hitch.

Give me the keys, the black said.

The old man drew and shot twice and hit both dogs in the neck. They caved heavily on the gravel. The rope leash went limp. The black looked around for a long second, like the dogs were still alive. He was all eyes and teeth. The rain dripped from the deep seams of the old man's face.

Pick up your dogs, the old man said.

The black was wide-eyed. He dropped the leash and backed into a burn barrel with his hands raised. He couldn't keep his mouth closed.

Pick them up and go, the old man said.

The black walked over to where the dogs lay flat. He took one in each arm. The fur was wet and long and smeared with the grit from the alley. He ran and walked away, comfortable with neither.

The old man looked at the pipe wrench and then looked at Walt.

Bronze Star? he said.

Walt drove just to drive, off through the green cornfields, where the furrows fell down with the curve of the earth. He took tractor roads and crossed overfull creeks on one-lane bridges and smoked a joint when the clouds came tilting from the east and the rain blew in sheets, even though the sun was hard in his eyes and lay down the shadows of fence posts. He held the smoke until none came out, and soon his eyes narrowed and the river in his head flowed until it met bigger rivers with currents that broke white over rocks and all water became other water. He unplugged the cell phone and stowed it in the glove compartment and drove the afternoon away, listening to old radio songs and singing many, "We got to get out of the place if it's the last thing we ever do," taking Route 1 into Papineau County, where Mexicans in straw cowboy hats stooped in melon fields, muddy to their thin waists, cutting the fruit from the vines with long knives. He stopped at a roadhouse near Saint Marie and bought two six-packs of Miller Lite and drove out Sugar Island Road and watched the sky above the river trees turn pink and gray.

The Vietnamese were building cinder-block storm sewers along Route 9 so the road to Khe Sanh wouldn't wash out for the war tourists. They shut down the lane by laying rocks on the broken asphalt, small boulders brought up from the river, where sampans hauled gravel against the current. Motor scooters shot around the van, weaving between the boulders, some carrying anesthetized pigs in long baskets, watermelons tied off with coarse rope, even families of three. The van driver honked the horn. The guide sat beside him, four long hairs growing from a mole on his cheek, and cursed the motor scooters with his hands. They were heading back to Hue. Old deuce and a halves filled with gravel trundled past the massed scooters. Tom poked his shoulder.

You remember any of this? he said.

No.

Nothing? You can't recognize anything?

It don't match my memories.

Tom looked at him and Walt stared out the window. The kid was bugging him with questions.

If he glanced fast, Vietnam was all the same. The heat and the red dust were there with the smell of urine and rotten fish. He still sweat straight salt and felt like he floated and never truly walked. The dust hardened upon his skin when the sweat dried, and he believed it was a tan. He choked in the wind. His eyes burned and ran, but he never stopped seeing. Old women with duck feet squatted on roadsides, selling warm Cokes while their husbands lay smiling upon hammocks strung in dark bamboo hootches. Men shod in tire-tread sandals irrigated rice paddies with roped buckets. Little boys without pants herded water buffalo across broken roads with droving sticks. And the dusk came suddenly, the white heat subsiding to a long redness and then a darkness not truly dark because of the big moon.

Walt waited these first days for the bad things the way he remembered they'd come. Riding in a convoy from Phu Bai to Dong Ha when mortars rained down from a hill of pine and scrub, the gunners so close that he could hear the rounds leaving the tubes, the gasoline trucks igniting and men running ablaze for the rice paddies, where farmers turned VC, pulling rifles from the assholes of water buffalo. Through many ambushes, he'd wondered how they hid the rifles. But nothing happened now. The Vietnamese stood on the roadsides, waving water bottles at the van, unsmiling like cats, their conical hats shadowed on the dust the old women swept outside tin hootches, where inside pots boiled over. One dollar, you buy from me, one dollar.

He was here, but the war was somewhere else. He walked the firebases where he'd slept in igloo bunkers and the rockets had slammed the earth. He saw nothing but the old sandbags twisted with the red earth. He'd blamed a lifetime of booze, three wives, and a dead son on Vietnam. Now he was here, walking the ground, but he couldn't find it.

For thirty-three years, I just thought it was this place that fucked me up, he thought.

You get ambushed on this road? Tom said.

Maybe, Walt said.

He glanced out of both windows, squinting to block Tom's reflection. He was the young man now. Wide shoulders, thin waist, just muscle and bone. He was up every morning at 4:30, running the stairs for an hour, doing push-ups in sets of a hundred, and the Vietnamese women watched him like a movie star. They patted Walt's stomach and called him happy Buddha.

I just can't get my bearings, he said, This place is so different, but it smells the same. I can't say at all. It's weird being here with just the gooks.

You ever see the NVA? Tom said.

One time, he said.

Walt stared through the side window at the red dust swirling down from the thin pines along the ridge. The workers molded the cinder blocks on the roadside, wearing tire-tread sandals and pith helmets. Some squatted in the shade and smoked cigarettes. The pith helmets were all gook, like the sandals made from old tires. They were all he recognized of the old DMZ. Con Thien and Gio Linh were rubber-tree farms. The Rockpile was a gravel quarry. The government grew coffee at Khe Sanh. The country was green again, filled with pine and small oaks, bushes and wildflowers, and nothing about the land west of Dong Ha reminded him of the war he carried behind his forehead. The scorched earth. The bare land. The thick dust kicked up from convoys while they snaked the roads between the firebases and took mortar fire from hills known only by numbers. But the helmets and sandals were real and they were what he'd seen when the illumination rounds went up at Con Thien the night the NVA massed around the wire and he got the Bronze Star for shooting at shadows.

Tom spit tobacco juice into an empty water bottle.

What sends you back? Tom said.

Shut up, Walt thought. Just sit and be goddamned quiet.

They came to Hue while the rain misted the pine hills. Later that night, Walt sat drinking alone in the hotel bar, where the massage girls lingered in the doorway, singing Britney Spears songs. They wore white shorts without panties, tight bébé-*doll T-shirts, and sang perfect English to the bootlegged CDs. They didn't call out to him like they had in the old days. That was a joke with them, the long-time, short-time, the number-one fucky sucky. They'd all seen the war movies on HBO. You VC. They laughed. No, you VC. The girls looked and waited, knowing these middle-aged American vets would pull out a twenty for old time's sake after five Tiger beers. Sometimes they smiled without showing teeth. Tom was sleeping in the room. He wouldn't drink in the heat. He had to get up and run.*

The Perfume River flowed past the bar in the moonlight and he did not know if the river or the bar smelled of mildew. He looked for a current, the eddy water of Illinois rivers when it swirled around bridge piers, but the river was calm. There were the lines left by the sampans that passed in the night, heading toward the Citadel, where John Tyne from Watega High School died in April 1968 and Barry Baron lost both legs outside the Thoung Tu Gate but made a million dollars after opening a Ford dealership. The sampans played radio music, American voices dubbed over an electronic beat, and the water went very still soon after they broke it. Earlier that day, he'd seen the bullet holes in the walls of the old city and touched the ones he could reach. Wrinkled women in conical hats had followed him, forever selling bottles of mineral water. When the marines attacked Hue, he'd waited in Dong Ha to fly back to Okinawa, then the world. Artillery rounds chased him and Hill down the runway while they ran for the gate of the C-130, the air force loadmaster yelling over the prop blast to ditch their seabags. Sitting at the bar now, he still felt his shineless boots hitting the air and saw Hill's wide smile and wagging tongue. You better run, maggot, Hill said, mocking the DIs at MCRD. Run he did. So far away. Beyond the sun, even past where the water and the sky fused and the earth curved forever downward. Life began now, he thought, when he jumped upon the gate and crawled into the fuselage, puking the last red dust from the DMZ, and Hill gave him the thumbs-up and they both smiled like fat pimps. You ever coming back, maggot? Fuck no. How about for a gook princess who will screw you harder than Ali McGraw on speed? Fuck no. The plane lifted straight up into the white sky and they heard the last artillery rounds leave small craters below, and that day was the first day of their long lives.

I'm back, Hill. I'm sitting right now in a bamboo bar, waiting for a drink. Too bad we never got to run Hue City. Too goddamned bad. There'd of been trouble. The girls will knock you back flat and not one of them knows what Prozac is. Not a one. I just wish I'd of known it thirty-three years ago. God, how I shit right in my mess kit and kept on eating.

He watched the hotel lights bleed upon the river when she came from the shadows, wearing the ao dai, *the long white dress and pants, her bikini underwear visible and low on her tiny hips. She walked behind the bar. He touched her in his thoughts and she moved through the dark as if she felt his hands. The girl smiled, her eyes and mouth painted upon her face. He felt himself tumble. He breathed with trouble. She handed him a menu of whiskies and brandies, then told him they only stocked Johnnie Walker Black.*

She was the idea he had about women but never once found. The dream of baring them your soul while they looked at you with soft dark eyes, feeling your pain more than understanding it, ready to let you bury it deep inside them. He was full of hate, he'd tell her. A hate like fire. Maybe just red-hot stones now, but once it had burned as if napalm in those mountains while he built the road all the way to the A Shau Valley, the road Charlie would use when he hit Hue City during the Tet Offensive. He hated his three wives, the young dumb one who'd Dear Johnned him when he was pushing down the thin pine trees along the Perfume River with his bulldozer, scraping the red clay into dust that caked his pores. The one that got too smart for him, even if he met her when she served drinks in a bunny outfit down in Bloomington, living in her AMC Pacer, but she got a real estate license and started making money when his father's business was failing. It wasn't because of him, he kept telling himself. Not him at all. Then Sherry, the barfly he picked up one night and kept for six years, a daughter she'd had at fourteen stuck away in a reform school north of Chicago, but the times were good—a party without a thing to celebrate, long nights at Fat Rats and cold shots of Jack Daniel's and cocaine lines on the bar after last call, when Pete locked out the unknowns with three dead bolts per door. The party lasted real good until the money got tight and he caught her sucking the neighbor kid off when he was home on leave from the navy. He opened up the garage door and saw her kneeling on a carpet sample, and he went crazy, chasing them through the alley puddles with a pipe wrench. Now there was Patty, the last stop, the end of the dreaming.

He watched the Vietnamese girl look around the bar. Her long black hair was tied behind her small head by a silk bow. Her face made him think of cats sleeping among white flowers.

I came here, he said, to start over again.

She made a face because she did not understand. He spoke slower. She nodded, her eyes like flowers in the wind.

I was here thirty-three years ago. When I go back this time, things are going to be different.

She smiled.

My name is Tuyen.

Mine is Walter.

She poured the scotch in the glass. The massage girls watched from the doorway. He wondered if they were all used to smelling the mold. She turned up the stereo.

Walt didn't like the music. He wanted to talk, tell her that he'd built a road from this river far into the A Shau Valley.

What do you think of the war? he said. Of us veterans coming back?

She sang the American songs and looked at the massage girls, and they all laughed.

Where did you learn English? he said.

I watch MTV on the satellite. Here in hotel.

She danced and grinned. Walt lit a cigarette and realized he couldn't remember Hill's face.

Let's get this party going, she said.

Walt pulled up beside his garage, where the water dripped from the cistern and surged out the gutter spout. The rains had passed two hours ago and the clouds were vague enough that the stars burned through and made the alley glow white. He saw her computer light in the bedroom upstairs, webbed in the window glass. It was past midnight. He parked the truck in the gravel space, pulled the shift lever into neutral, and pushed down the brake. He glowed green from the dash and knew he was drunk by the way he stared at the headlight beams boring into the wet trees. His chin wagged. He drew on his cigarette as if he were inflating himself, then shut down the engine and got out before remembering he'd left on the lights. He pushed them off through the open door. With the bright starlight, the night did not seem darker without the headlamps. He looked at the windshield, remembering the bird that had flown into it after dusk, dying and sliding down the wet glass to lie along the wiper blade. Then he turned around and started taking a leak.

Tom came from around the garage and walked up the alley. Walt zipped himself and leaned against the tailgate. He was mournfully drunk. It took him three tries to find the cigarette with the lighter.

"Are you all right?" Tom said.

"I'm all right."

"What's going on?" Tom said.

"The old man dead yet?"

"You know he ain't."

"Then I guess I shouldn't ask you for a loan."

"What's that supposed to mean?"

"I'd contest his will. I earned that money."

"I don't even know what happened between us."

Walt leaned, looking at the empty street beyond the Clark station. He missed his mouth with the cigarette.

"You were causing problems between me and my wife over there."

Tom looked at him, then looked away.

"Every time you checked those E-mails at the hotel," Walt said, "you came back lying. Patty never said what you told me she wrote."

"Why didn't you ever check them yourself? Shit, you told me the whole time how crazy she was. She sent those E-mails asking us how our whores were."

Walt was leaning slowly sideways.

"I ain't your father," he said.

"Why you doing this?"

"Just go your way."

"So your son's gone and I'm gone, too."

"Throw that up in my face."

Walt's eyes went dark. He flipped the cigarette at Tom and it bounced off his shoulder. "Fuck you," he said.

Tom looked at him and walked away, slow steps through the

alley puddles. Walt finished his cigarette and searched his pockets for another.

Teddy sat on the old man's lap and laughed while he made an ape face. He jammed his tongue against his bottom lip and Teddy slapped the air. He did monkeys, bears, even dogs. Walt slumped on the couch, dirty from the crawl spaces, drinking the old man's Pabst. The can was cold against his calluses. He stared hollow-eyed at the television set, where the last marines were leaving the rooftop of the U.S. embassy in Saigon. He remembered the first day of boot camp, the DI ranting, that drawl in his head like a hangover: The men who have stood on these footprints before you maggot cocksuckers have never given ground because they knew that a live marine with a rifle can resist anything. What does make me worthy? Walt once thought. He looked over at the old man and Teddy, then the Medal of Honor behind framed glass on the wall.

Michalski, Walter Tedor

Rank and organization: Staff Sergeant, U.S. Army, Company B, 505th Infantry, 82d Airborne Division. Place and date: Near Sainte-Mère-Eglise, France, 6 June 1944. Entered Service at: Watega, Ill. Born: 9 October 1918, Saint Marie, Ill. G.O. No.: 67, 21 June 1945.

Citation:

In the early morning of 6 June 1944, near Sainte-Mère-Eglise, assembling 18 men after the parachute drop into Carenten, Staff Sergeant Michalski's detachment was pinned down by a German .88-mm gun and two machine guns. Arming himself with an M1 rifle, a grenade

> *launcher, and a number of rifle and hand grenades, he left his detachment in position and advanced alone, under fire, up the slope toward the hedgerow that concealed the enemy emplacements. Struck on the head and knocked down by a glancing machine-gun bullet, Staff Sergeant Michalski, in spite of his painful wounding and enemy fire at close range, continued up the hill, throwing grenades every few steps. Despite the stream of enemy machine-gun fire, which barely missed him, Staff Sergeant Michalski reached the vantage point and silenced the .88mm gun with a well-placed rifle grenade and, throwing hand grenades, knocked out two machine guns, again being painfully wounded. Staff Sergeant Michalski's heroic leadership and indomitable courage in alone silencing these enemy weapons inspired his men to great effort and cleared the way for subsequent units to advance and reach their objectives.*

Walt put his beer down on the end table and stumbled up to attention. His knees quaked. The helicopter hovered while the last marine climbed aboard, pausing with his rifle to look over the rusty rooftops of Saigon. The old man grunted through his nose and tickled Teddy. The boy convulsed from laughter and mocked the ape face, his tongue against the wrong lip. The old man was showing him how, when Walt staggered to the television and pissed all over the screen. He laughed darkly. Semper fi, *do or die. The urine ran down the glass; the carpet sponged it. He was floating. On the screen Walt watched the old man shake his head quietly, as if he were part of the newscast, then send Teddy from the room. The kid ran out crying, his legs awobble.*

If you ain't a sack of goddamned shit, the old man said.

4

Jimmy tipped the beer bottle up and he drank long when Tom came out on the porch. The night was warm and filled with stars and locust sounds from the river woods across the curbless street. His dog, Jack, lay watching the fireflies reel beneath the willow tree and his eyes darted and ears perked when more illuminated above the neighbor's woodpile. He growled in low tones and Jimmy dropped a hand to stroke his black head. A cocklebur was matted with the long fur beneath his ear and soon Jimmy was trying to work it free. Tom sat on a lawn chair and stared at the black paint staining his fingernails. Jimmy drank, then wiped his mouth with his bare arm.

"Two planes rammed the World Trade Center. They don't know anything else," he said.

"Yeah."

Jimmy leaned the chair so the back rested against the clapboard siding. They sat without the porch light.

"You want me to kill it?" Tom said.

"There isn't much more to know."

Tom went inside and turned off the television. He came back with two beers and sat down.

"We're at war now."

"With a hundred guys."

Tom said nothing.

"Just don't start talking about sending in the Eighty-second Airborne and the marines. I was at Jarhead's all day. I can't hear any more of it."

"I'd go back as a private."

"You're out on bad paper, Jane. You're down with the bed wetters and the faggots."

"You wouldn't want to go?"

"Where?

"You're like a broad."

Jimmy shook his head in the darkness. The dog lost interest in the fireflies and laid his snout down along his forelegs.

"When we come through southern Iraq and saw all those bodies strewn across the desert, my squad leader, this Cracker from north Georgia named Mapes, looks at me and says, 'Ruell, these people are going to get us for shooting fish in a barrel. This ain't fighting; it's plain-assed killing.' We've been asking for this."

"Who are you to say that?"

"The guy who's letting you crash rent-free."

"Here's to you, jarhead."

"Just quit leaving the toilet seat up."

"She sure knew how to get in your head," Tom said.

"I said getting divorced will change you."

Tom rose and left the porch and walked around in front of his truck. He leaned against the grille. Jimmy looked over at him and laughed.

"You think you'll ever let your hair grow a little?" he said. "That lifer haircut scares women."

"I've always scared women."

Tom reached in the truck window and got a fresh pack of cigarettes. He opened them without watching himself. The wind smelled of rain and warm river mud.

"Walt told me to fuck off," he said.

"Let it go."

"He always said he wished I was his son."

"You haven't served him beer for the last eight years."

"No."

"Walt knows he's past the point of learning from his mistakes," Jimmy said.

Tom lit the cigarette and let the match flame until it burned his finger. Jimmy watched him and stroked the dog behind his ears.

"What made you bring him to Vietnam?"

"Because it was the last war we'll ever have."

"You're mad you were born too late."

Tom Jane shook his head. "You'd tell me if I was getting in your way here?" he said.

"Yeah. But I still wouldn't want you to leave. Let's head over to the Dam Tap and see how many women will ignore us."

"We're ignoring them tonight."

"Ain't possible, Jane."

"I know."

Tom got in the truck and had the engine started before Jimmy even rose from his chair. He thought of moving down the highway, driving fast, just looking out the window at the passing darkness while the tires rubbed the asphalt.

5

The Xanex took Patty away around midnight and left her curled on the bed. The doctor doubled her dosage and she lost interest in the computer. She stared at walls, gone to the blank spaces. Before she went cold, she looked silently at Walt and he watched her eyes glaze like wet glass. It was all fine with him. She was quiet. He chatted the long nights in an AOL room called Vietnam Veterans. There were guys with screen names like sinloivc, miaintheworld, usmcgrunt, justbuzin. The names were like second tries at vanity plates. He was just wmichalski. Most guys typed in the old phrases from their war: *Fug it. There it is. Hanoi Jane is a spitter?* They held contests. Who could cuss like a lifer? What were all the meals in C rations, and which ones didn't have the canned fruit? How many bunks in a squad bay at MCRD?

One night, earlover and gookhumper got into it about what R and R town had the best boom-boom girls, Bangkok or Manila. Stonecold typed that he got the best action right in-country from the Red Cross girls, the biscuit bitches. Doorgunner said stonecold'd never learned the way of the Nam. Round-eyed pussy was overrated and too expensive. He typed, *Still can't get it up unless the eyes slant and the snatch is sideways. . . . Remember the silk rope? . . . There are things we never would have known without the Nam.* Everybody agreed except stonecold. *I always felt like a child molester with a gook . . . no hair . . . made me beaucoup nervous . . . went right to chaplain Charlie.*

He sat on-line smoking cigarettes and looking out the window at the dark hickory trees. The guys were typing about what they'd need as middle-aged men if the U.S. called them back for combat. *A nap around three in the afternoon. . . . No fugging humping before ten in the morning. . . . No more military time. . . . Pack mules for the rucksacks. . . . Happy hour after a firefight and, hell yes, Charlie can drink right with us, better Charlie than an army draftee, rather have a sister in the whorehouse than a brother in the army reserve. . . . Fug it, one firefight a week, only twenty rounds for Charlie, twenty for us. . . . How about no firefights with Charlie, we have a fishing derby instead?*

Walt got to know a guy named skysoldier. He lurked in the room like Walt, typing little, maybe looking out windows at the same dark hickories. They sent instant messages, small greetings, some talk about cars and motorcycles and shotguns, but never about Vietnam. That night, the instant-message window popped up, a great surprise, Walt thought, like a letter from the world thirty years ago. Skysoldier was divorced, with two kids who hardly talked to him, an avid bird hunter from Sioux Falls, South Dakota, who told Walt the skies out there were black with cock pheasant, but always stopped short of a hunting invitation.

Lighting out, wmich, skysoldier typed.

Lighting out?

Bought land in Idaho. I'm talking early retirement from the state police. I'm short here. Color me gone come morning.

Didn't know you were a cop.

I didn't, either. For thirty years. Just did it.

You keeping your computer.

Yes, wmich. E-mail only. No more skysoldier, no more Vietnam anything. Sick of it. I'm tdenny now.

Why, tdenny?

I'm more interested in our future, wmich. Not our past. Spent thirty years talking about twelve months in Asia. Nothing more to say.

No shit.

Wouldn't shit my favorite turd, wmich.

Write soon, tdenny.

Might be awhile. Got to build a log cabin. I ordered it as a kit. I'll be sleeping in my camper until then.

Good luck.

Our future, wmich. We still got some left.

Walt signed off and snuffed his cigarette. Patty was coiled on the bed, lost in medicated slumber. He looked around the room, the darkness visible after the computer shut down. He was tired and sleep was impossible. His body felt like piled gravel. Fatigue set in behind his forehead and his eyes burned and hardened in their sockets.

His father brought the old TV from the bungalow over to the plumbing shop. He put it on a stand between the two long tables where they bent sheet metal into ductwork and he watched the fights on Friday nights with his guys. They filled a rubber garbage can with Pabst and ice and grilled steaks and halved onions in the alley, potatoes wrapped in foil. Lou Boudreau worked the grill—he'd cooked horse meat the same way in Stalag Luft 3—the skin around his eyes scarred purple from old burns. He'd flown a B-17 and lost his flight goggles even before the plane got hit somewhere outside of Hamburg, the flak taking the wings in the same second, and the fuselage catching fire but holding steady in the dark sky for an odd minute. Lou didn't know he'd lost them. His leather flying hat and oxygen mask had saved most of his face from the fire, but the flames scorched him around the eyes. He never saw himself jump, pull the rip cord, land on a barn roof, or the old Krauthead that bayed him with a shotgun before the SS came.

That week, North Vietnam had released the fliers from the Hanoi Hilton. All the old men watched the tin-shop TV as the guys hobbled off the C-130 in the Philippines, wearing those blue uniforms, smiling and bleary-eyed but seeming unsure of how to look at things.

Whenever Walt talked about Vietnam, they'd change the subject or tell him about World War II. Nothing ever compared. Walt told them that Vietnam soldiers saw more sustained combat during their 365-day rotations than most infantrymen during World War II. They lived in fear longer. The old men laughed and asked him where was the Anzio beachhead in Vietnam. They showed it like a trump card. There was Ia Drang and Hue, but worse, the never knowing who was what. That was a cliché now. He hated even saying it. They still wanted to know where the Anzio beachhead was. Then Walt stopped arguing.

It was worse in the Pacific. That was the first thing they said. None of them knew why the pilots didn't kill themselves, rather than be taken prisoner by a gook. That's what they all would have done. Duane Mau knew a guy who'd survived the Bataan death march and then was worked half to death in a Japanese steel mill until VJ day. He lived right over in Saint Marie and grew Christmas trees and pumpkins. Duane wondered why he hadn't shot himself, either. He ain't been fit for much since he come home. Won't sit at the same table where rice is served. We worked to-

gether over at General Foods right after the war, shoveling grain off boxcars. We'd fun him a bit, you know, mock-talk Nip and watch him go to pieces.

Boudreau had a bad eye from the burn. It slid toward his nose, then his temple, always wandering. Take the cock out of your eye and put it in your pants, the guys would say. The grill was a fifty-five-gallon drum halved by a cutting torch, and the rain steamed when it hit the sides. Boudreau turned the steaks with homemade tongs. The flames hissed from the water running out of the halved onions.

Walt and Lou stood just inside the back door, out of the rain. Boudreau turned the steaks quickly and stepped backward.

They could have at least tried escaping, Lou said. That made us look bad.

The gooks kept them alone in cells for years.

We tunneled all the time. The Krauts found one, we had three more. We drove them crazy like that. If one man got out, all the Kraut officers went to Russia.

There was no way for our guys.

You couldn't light a match in the tunnels. The air was too foul. But we kept digging. Sometimes using a mess tin. They'd collapse on us, but we learned from it.

How were they going to dig alone?

The problem was ventilation. You'd get dizzy down there. We tried using airholes and poking up pieces of pipe, but the Krauts smelled the air. Things started turning around when we got some guys from West Virginia in the camp. They'd been miners before the Air Corps.

I don't think our guys saw much of each other.

That ain't an excuse. American officers got to be resourceful. Shit, we wired our tunnels to the damned camp and had lights to dig by. You just make your mind up and you do it.

They ever torture you guys?

Boudreau looked out at the rain blowing through the alley. Your duty is to escape, he said.

You blended in over in Europe.

They should have done something besides sit on their asses.

Walt watched his last morning in Watega County come through the pickup window. The darkness dissolved among the trees in the river woods and slipped down the horizon and the sun rose from the cornstalks white and burning and shapeless and the tree shadows appeared blurry on the grass. He called Shep inside from the gravel alley and the dog climbed over his thighs. He finished his coffee and pitched his cigarette butt out the window.

He was leaving it all today. He'd packed two garbage bags full of winter clothes when Patty was sleeping—ready with a Salvation Army donation story if she woke up—and hid them among his carpentry tools in the truck bed. He took the forty grand from behind the loose cinder block in the garage, the money nobody knew about, gotten from selling eight balls of cocaine to friends of friends at Fat Rat's and the USA Tap on Station Street, mostly long-haul truckers who dropped a thousand dollars at a time. *Shit runs down the miles, Walt.* He quit when his connection stopped answering his pager, a young guy with a spider tattooed on his neck, who sang in a band that covered Black Sabbath songs. He waited for the cops to come, looking over both shoulders from Christmas until past April, but nothing happened. Whatever tools were left from the plumbing business, he locked in the garage and then mailed the key to the old man's bungalow on Grant Street. No note, just the key. He wrote up a note saying that Patty could have the house, the sixteen hundred dollars in checking, and the 1992 Lincoln Town Car he'd bought at 32 percent after filing for bankruptcy.

The sun rose in the west when he passed the clay pits on Grand Army of the Republic Highway and left Watega County. The light came upon the fields in a sudden white flash. Shep sat on the bench seat and barked at the passing telephone poles lining the bar ditch. He would drive for the Mississippi River, where the fields gave way to wooded bluffs, and a man could go a full hour without seeing a closed stove factory. He might not make it to the Montana of his dreams and walk along prairie rivers like Jeremiah Johnson while the wind swept the tall grass and white mountains tore open the clouds, his belly fat on brown trout and venison. He'd drive until he found a piece of ground twenty grand might buy, then stop there, and be happy with the dream he got, because anywhere he landed, his father wouldn't know where to start looking.

Walt might come home when the old man was laid out in Klenzak's Funeral Home, his father wearing his one dark suit, the Medal of Honor around his neck, his face too white, his calloused hands folded with a rosary. He might breathe easy, maybe laugh while the old men who'd depended on the old man for a paycheck filed past the casket like it was a buffet dinner. None would have dry eyes when they saluted the medal, boot camp–sharp. Walt would shake their rough hands, strong from a lifetime gripping pipe wrenches, and swallow laughter while his mother cried into a wadded tissue and his sister added up the inheritance behind her forehead. He'd be happy, even smiling. It would all be done. He'd first dreamed this day when the Marine Corps discharged him back to the old man for a lifetime of digging sewer lines. He'd kept dreaming it whenever the old man looked at him like he'd meant to kill a half-retarded boy. The old man would be full of embalming fluid and he would've left the county and remade himself on a hilltop. What he'd become, he didn't know, but he'd be something different the day they buried the old man beneath a flat sheet of VA bronze.

6

The pigs came filing out of the semitrailer not minutes after the driver jackknifed and tipped over beneath the yellow flasher on 113. Dwight Baum was parked on a field road, reading *Soldier of Fortune* magazine, an article about how to train for hostage-rescue situations, when the big truck slowly took the curve and went over. He turned on his lights and blocked the road with his squad car and shoved the magazine beneath the seat. The driver climbed from the cab and waved that he was fine. The sky was clear and white. Dwight called for backup and an ambulance. Jerry Bowman laughed hard at him about the situation report. "Be careful of ambushes, commando. Them might be Arab pigs." Bowman had never let up with jokes after Dwight had proposed the Hall County Sheriff's Department start a counterterrorism unit. "It's a changing world," Dwight'd argued, "and we need to change with it." Bowman hadn't responded, just lit a second cigarette.

"You hear that on TV, Baum?" he said now.

The driver stood among the roadside weeds, pointing and shaking his head. He was a fat man with sunburned arms. Fifteen pigs were crossing the bar ditch to root in a dusty bean field. Dwight looked at him and then looked at the pigs shredding the bean leaves. The smell of pig manure came like water rising.

"How'd this happen?" he said.

The driver's face was two-toned, red and white. He looked back at his truck, flat on its side. He laughed real low.

"It's the strangest goddamned thing," he said. "We better get on. That'll catch fire."

"I don't smell gas."

"I've had them light up in the lot. Just sitting there."

Dwight took the pump shotgun from the rack and hung a bandolier of shells over his arm. He walked with the weapon at port arms. The sweat stung his eyes behind his sunglasses. Winged grasshoppers popped up from the roadside grass. The driver followed him to the edge of the bar ditch and spat.

"What you going to do with that shotgun?" the driver said.

"Keep the pigs from destroying Duane Mossman's field."

The driver shook his head.

"Warning shots don't mean dick to a pig."

Dwight said nothing and stared out at the field through his sunglasses.

"I just filled that truck with gas an hour ago," the driver said.

"You wait for the backup."

"Shit," he said.

The driver started running away from the truck. He hoofed it in cowboy boots, tight jeans with a flare, his waist fat rolling over his belt. He wanted to go faster, but his body wouldn't let him.

Dwight ran into the field and the bean leaves were spotted

yellow and came past his knees. Dust clouds rose where the pigs rooted between the furrow lines. They gurgled and snorted. Some wallowed on their backs and kicked about their forelegs. Dwight chambered a shell and fired a warning shot, but the pigs continued rooting. No birds sprang from the hedge trees by the creek. He chased one small pig, covered in sandy dust, but stopped and breathed hard, wondering what he'd do if he caught one. Then he started shooting the pigs, pointing and firing without drawing a bead. The double-ought buckshot halved their heads and the swine collapsed heavily in the field dust. The crops were weltered with gore. He worked the pump and squeezed the trigger.

The boys were wet from the showers, their skin blushing from the draft in the locker room. There was a lanky black kid named Johnnie Green, who walked like a rooster and took showers in socks and cleats. Beside him were two boys, and they looked cruelly at Dwight through their wet bangs. The football team called Dwight the Package Peeker, and he was late folding the brown towels from the dryer. He'd taken the job after his father died of a heart attack at the Firestone factory, a guy who'd spent twenty-five years on nights and liked it. Coach Barclay leaned against the lockers with his arms folded across his chest. He chewed gum and glared at Dwight while he folded the towels. He wore tight polyester shorts that snapped below his gut.

Johnnie Green looked at Dwight. His teeth rattled. Hurry up, Peek, my balls is blue, he said.

The boys laughed, heavyset boys from the country, who pushed the coach across the field on the blocking sled. They had first called him Package Peeker, but now they just called him Peek. All went quiet when Barclay blew his whistle.

What's the hold up, Peek? the coach said.

Dwight went on folding. One long fold, then halve the brown towel and stack it on the metal shelf.

You thinking about a dick you'd like to have? the coach said. There's places in Sweden where they can fix you right up. Shit, I bet you can speak a good while about the difference between dicks.

The boys howled. Johnnie Green did his touchdown dance, the cleats tapping the tiles. Dwight counted the stacked towels by twos. He recounted and nodded his head.

Ready, he said.

How about a dick like Green's, Peek? the coach said. That'd be something to have. Goddamn Green has to halve that thing just to put his pants on. I bet you're wondering if maybe Green's mom don't know God personally.

Johnnie Green pointed to his testicles and smiled toothily at Dwight. The boys laughed and filed past the window, taking their towels. Johnnie kept looking at Dwight and soon started singing along with his dance: Big balls, ya hee, big balls, talking to me. I got some big balls, bigger than a tree. My big balls, they almost bigger than me.

Dwight sat on the stool behind the window and watched him dance long after the coach had left and the boys stopped laughing. Johnnie Green was the only black kid in the high school, and the coach left him alone about showering in socks and cleats. He scored touchdowns and never talked to white girls. When Green was done, Dwight went upstairs to help old Pug Haslett clean the high school, buff the hallways until they reflected everything upside down, then buy his mother cigarettes on the way home, GPC menthol 100's.

Sheriff Tim Bertrand sat in the varnished oak swivel chair and Jerry Bowman sat laughing on the edge of his desk. Dwight stood with his hat in his hand and glanced down at the picture of Bertrand's wife, Krissy, in a neon green thong and a Santa hat. She was like that and he wanted you to know it. Bertrand took a cigarette from his pocket while Bowman gagged from laughter. Six months ago, Bertrand had been just another deputy, but he won the election by fifty-two votes; then he started calling Dwight "Peek," even though he'd gone to school in Kewanee. He looked out the window and lit the cigarette.

"Why'd you shoot them pigs, Peek?" he said.

"They were ruining Mossman's field," Dwight said.

"A half acre of beans is cheaper than them pigs. That hog farmer's got a lawsuit."

"They could have run in the road and caused accidents."

"That's why you block it off."

"I used my best judgment."

Bowman snorted and said "Shit" to himself. He swallowed. His eyes were running.

"Peek here couldn't find his ass with both hands," he said.

"At ease, Jerry," Bertrand said.

"Shit, Peek. Maybe them was Arab pigs. You're damned lucky they weren't Vietcong pigs. You'd of had beaucoup problems. I watched them VC pigs eat the nose off a papa-sanh. No lie."

"That's enough, Jerry," Bertrand said.

"Did you use your counterterrorist tactics, Peek? I hope *Soldier of Fortune* magazine didn't fail you in the heat of battle."

"Jerry, get the hell out of here," Bertrand said.

Bowman stood heavily from the desk. He pulled his pants up around his waist. His khaki uniform was wrinkled, but the fake creases sewn through the pockets held. He looked at

Dwight, then Bertrand. "They'll laugh at us for ten years over this," he said. Then he threw his hands up and walked out.

Bertrand laughed woodenly. He snuffed the cigarette in a pop can.

"The shit of it is, Peek, I don't have the manpower to even suspend you."

Dwight took it all, afraid to hate him with his eyes. Being a sheriff's deputy was as good as it got for him. He knew that. The army hadn't wanted him because of a bad reaction to a bee sting. He'd sent off applications for the ATF three times and never heard back. He even ran a classified in the back of *Soldier of Fortune*, advertising himself as a security specialist, but nothing came of it. If this ended, it was back to guarding the gold at the Jostens in Peoria, where they made class rings, walking the hallways with pepper spray while the black guys in shower caps emptied the garbage cans. They reeked of dope smoke and mumbled rent-a-pig.

Dwight saw Jenny in the Eagle parking lot without the kids. She opened the hatchback and propped it open with a broom handle, then put in the grocery bags. Not a pretty girl. She was slightly overweight, divorced, with two kids, and managed the office for Steve Parr's State Farm Insurance. A sure bet, he'd once thought. She wasn't going anywhere, and the kids spent weekends with their father. Then six months ago, she'd called him and said it was over. When he asked her why, she told him he didn't want to know, said it was only her opinion anyway.

He parked by the bank and watched her. She closed the hatchback, paused, and looked across the street at the Wal-Mart as if the building weren't there. She crossed her arms and stared past it all. Just before she got in the car, she looked at the Wal-Mart again and sighed. Dwight figured she was lonely and that he could work that.

She drove off, her tires needing air. He looked at his watch, lit a cigarette, then tailed her down Main Street, past the grain elevator converted into an antiques mall. He waited for her to turn onto First, where the street skirted a big empty field, then hit the lights and pulled her over. He popped a mint. He walked up to the passenger window with his hand on his Glock. The cop act never turned her on, but he kept trying.

"I want to see your license for being so hot," he said.

Jenny looked up at him. She had a double chin, acne scars on her cheeks. She pushed her glasses back up her nose and shook her head.

"Did I do something?" she said.

"Besides make me pant?" he said. "You can't do that to a police officer. I'm on duty."

"You do this again," she said, "I'm calling Tim Bertrand."

She put the small car in gear and drove away. He stood awhile in the street, watching even after she'd gone. The sky was low and white.

He drove home to the trailer he rented two miles off 37 West, a place that deer hunters once used for warming themselves between the morning and late-afternoon hunts. The country was all sand and pine trees, and milkweed and thistle filled the bar ditches, and late on hot nights he smelled the soybean-processing plant ten miles away in Cherry. The trailer had three rooms and four windows, and if he stood on his bed, he could touch both walls with outstretched arms. There was a big-screen TV, forty-two inches, so wide that he set it on the kitchen table and watched it from the back of his bedroom. He owned every war movie amazon.com sold, and sometimes he logged on the site and searched for more even when he knew there were none. He never watched them from the beginning, only certain scenes, and he held special guns for them all so he could imagine himself in the action. He liked the Russian roulette scene in *The Deer Hunter* the best, and he played with a Remington 870 pump while Robert De Niro asked the VC officer for three bullets instead of one. That would be the best weapon for the situation—if it was loaded with double-ought buckshot, he'd clear the room with three rounds. He watched the scene over many times and never quite understood how De Niro ended up spraying the room with an AK-47 after shooting the guy in the forehead. A man couldn't be that fast.

Outside, the dusk was hemming the skies gray above the fields. The darkness would come hot, without wind rattling the hickory leaves dried by the sun, a perfect night for training. He took off his uniform and put on black night-stalker fatigues. He painted tiger stripes across his face with a camouflage stick, dark green, light green. He tied a black rag around his head, laced up his jungle boots, then snapped the knife scabbard to his ankle. He studied himself in the full-length mirror, folding his arms across his chest, drawing his eyes. Someday the department would need him like this. A hostage situation at the high school. Gunmen holding the tellers at the Tiskilwa Bank. He'd be ready, there before the sheriff even called him, getting precise head shots with his Glock .45, then clearing the room with double-ought buckshot. Nobody would laugh after that.

He walked outside and sat on the stoop. The boys usually came right after dark, walking down the dirt road off the state road, skinny teenagers in blue jeans and odd pieces of military surplus bought at the Hall County Gun Show. He was training them in the hickory grove behind the trailer, where a creekbed slanted through from the fields. Back in April, after a week of rains, he'd caught them shooting frogs in the creek with an air rifle, baiting them with flies made of knotted thread, tied off to a stick, then popping them on the jump. They took turns, but Andy, the tall one, could really shoot. Russell had a bad tick and twitched too much for shooting straight. He was only along for something to do. They came five nights a week for Dwight to teach them how to shoot. He set up cardboard silhouettes he made from grocery-store boxes, placing them behind stumps and scrub bushes, then covering them with red T-shirts for the terrorists, white shirts for the hostages, the way the *Soldier of Fortune* article instructed. They took turns running the footpath, pointing and firing, and hoped to hit the right-color T-shirt. "Instinct shooting," the article called it. Delta Force trained this way, even the British SAS. But tonight, the training would be different. He'd gotten the $348 laser sight from the U.S. Cavalry Store on-line, and a gunsmith had attached it to his new H&K .45 USP, the preferred pistol of the navy SEALs. The round hit wherever he pointed the red beam.

Dwight walked down the porch steps when Andy and Jack came from the woods, outlined against the fading light. They were muddy, wet past their thighs, and moved clumsily through the pine scrub. Their faces were blackened with shoe polish. Jack aimed a .38 Special at unknown targets in the sky, his eyes spinning in different directions. Andy carried an old over-and-under, his legs almost longer than the shotgun's barrel.

"All I got's bird shot," he said. "Number six."

"That won't do nothing but stun them," Dwight said. "You got to train for real."

"My grandpa didn't have nothing else."

"What is the range of an excuse?"

"Goddamn buckshot's six dollars for five shells."

Dwight looked at Jack. He took the .38 from his hand and aimed at the trailer. The front sight post was bent. The pistol grip looked like it had been used to hammer nails.

"What the hell you going to hit with this?" he said.

"I figure I'd shoot right, since it's bent the other way."

"You're not going to be thinking about pulling right in a firefight."

"Yeah."

"Yeah?" Dwight said.

"Yes, sir."

"Discipline will keep us alive," Dwight said. "Because someday the shit could really hit the fan. The government could try to take our guns. We'd have to hide in these woods."

"From the mayor?" Andy said.

"No, the feds."

The boys looked at him with their mouths open. "Why would a baseball team take our guns?" Andy said.

"No, the federal government."

Jack nodded and looked at Dwight's new pistol, snapped in a shoulder holster.

"We taking turns with it," Andy said.

Dwight looked up between the pine branches, where the darkness seemed to run in the wind.

"You'll fuck it all up," he said.

7

The house Walt bought on the hilltop was an old hunting lodge, and it looked across the bottomland to the river trees, where the leaves yellowed and hardened and sounded like rain in the wind. The river was brown beneath the shade of the trees and fed the Mississippi sixty miles away, and in the sun the water broke white around the rocks where the channels were shallow and swiftly moving. The wind gusted from behind the shacklike house, over the pine forest and the narrow creek, and the field dust it raised powdered Shep's black fur and made the dog turn gray. The rotten clapboards of the lodge were also dusty, like the one window that was not boarded, and the creek that ran down the hillside turned muddy from the dust and it layered the tar roof and the pickup's hood, so that in the mornings he saw the tracks left by raccoons and feral cats.

He did nothing the first three days but walk the hilltop with the dog, a handkerchief over his nose and mouth against the dust, and look at the deer tracks marring the brown needles in the dark pines, the bird nests crotched in ancient hickory trees beside the ruins of deer stands; often staring at the sky while he trod down rocky draws, his eyes bleary from the dust, hoping for thick rain clouds to hood the country, but none would come. He thought of the work before him. The house had been painted blue long ago and there were streaks of it left on the gray clapboards. The roof sagged from the weight of winter snows and the cisterns were thinned by rust and filled with dead leaves.

The old man who sold him the hilltop had once hunted these woods. His hands were long and veiny and chapped red like his face. He stood like his hips bothered him and pointed things out. He'd planted a glade of sorghum down the ridge for pheasant and quail and kept a quarter acre of popcorn near the river, where, come autumn, he worked his dogs through the furrow lines after grouse. Beyond the pines, there was an oak grove where the creek widened against the field side, and there he had four deer blinds in the trees. But he wouldn't be asking permission to hunt here; he made that clear right away. "The cold wind," he said, "gets in my ears and I hear it howling for six days. The shittingest thing. Doctor just gives me medicine that's like a half pint of whiskey in two pills." He wiped his nose with his shirtsleeve and folded the envelope of bills the best he could before shoving it into his pants pocket. Walt signed the papers on the truck hood. The old man spat.

"Where you from again?"

"Calumet City," Walt lied. "I retired from U.S. Steel."

"Chicago boy?"

"Close."

"I got to ask you," he said.

Walt handed him the papers. The dust had glazed the man's lips.

"Why you paying twenty grand to live in Hall County, Illinois?"

"I could drive around half my life looking for a place and spend all my money on gas."

"I hate to be an asshole," the man said, "but you look like you been doing just that."

Walt smiled vaguely. He scratched his beard. He looked away from the man and then looked back.

"I'd of fought you over that when I was younger," he said.

The man laughed.

"I wouldn't have said anything if I wasn't so old."

"The place just feels right."

"There's channel cat in the river. Large-mouth bass. Game's good. The water's clean. We never had the industry."

"A poor man's Montana."

"You could do a lot worse in Montana," the man said.

"You been there?"

"No," he said.

That night, Walt screened the porch with mosquito netting and lay smoking in the mooned heat. The birds came from the fields out east and sheered away over the pines. He listened to their calls become thin and lost to the wooded up-country while the wind swept the pines and rattled the brown-brier thicket. Shep lay beneath his surplus cot, wet from the creek and snapping at gnats, his black fur gummed from milkweed. It was good to be here, looking out at the hammered clouds stretching over the river. In the morning, he'd start work, set to it like wind twisting flames, and dig the foundation for a double-wide garage, where he'd winter until the country thawed and spring mud dried.

Then he'd order a log cabin from the company in California and have the lane graded and well rocked so the truck could deliver the kit, built the way the Marine Corps had taught him to scrape the gravel roads off Route 1 that went far into the A Shau Valley, the very roads the dinks took when they hit Hue City in 1968 and he and Hill were waiting in the rain at Dong Ha to fly far away forever and buy brand-new Pontiac GTOs with eight-track players and extra chrome strips down the sides. *Ain't gonna go home, are we, Walt? Hell no. Just going to drive, to drive, race those cars up and down Route One while the blue water hits the rocks and sprays up on the road.*

He'd start a woodworking shop in the garage this winter and sleep right next to his table saw, building gun cabinets and small shelves for trinkets, and travel to flea markets and sell his wares among strangers. He'd be a bearded man with a pickup full of wood-crafted objects and a dog who barked at silence and slept through electrical storms. But he couldn't be invisible. He knew that if people saw you more than three times, they wanted to know things about the life that got you this far. Walt would have a year of lonely work to think the stories through and have the right details all imagined so they stuck like cockleburs. He smoked another cigarette and drank canned beer wet from the cooler. *A man never rises again in the eyes of the people who watched him fall.* He rose and parted the netting and pitched the butt out in the dust and watched it flare and lapse.

Every Christmas Day, the old men played pinochle around the table the old man had made. The basement was warmed by kerosene heaters, lit with naked bulbs. A wool army blanket covered the unsanded wood and hung unevenly over the table sides. They took their cards and drank Schlitz from a can and drew on AC

Grenadiers like they had something. Uncle Katz had been a waist gunner on a B-17 and flown the Polesti raids and had yellow fingers from smoking Camel straights. Jack Baglarz, Aunt Sophie's stuttering husband, had driven a Sherman tank through the hedgerows outside Paris and been on line in the Ardennes the night the King Tigers broke the ancient beech trees in half. There was squint-eyed Uncle Wally, who'd fought his way inland on Guadalcanal with the first marines and taken a bamboo bayonet through the chest and then was made well enough to get gut-shot on the coral reef at Peleliu. The old man dealt first and called the games—rummy, straight gin, even hit when they got too drunk on Early Times to table scores. They never moaned. It was his basement and he signed their paychecks and had won the medal, making him their boss forever.

The basement steps ran down from the garage, and Walt sat upon them with his cousins John and Stanley, watching oil leak from the old man's Bel Air. They were Uncle Wally's boys, born a year apart, nervous kids that never spoke. John coughed but never had a cold. Stan stuttered and formed words like a cat trying to vomit. They lived according to Uncle Wally's moods in his wood-frame house on Sherman Street, which he ran like a marine barracks, making themselves invisible when he felt the bamboo bayonet gore his chest all over again. The boys were allowed no farther than these steps.

They heard their fathers without seeing them, their voices loud from the Schlitz. Uncle Wally always boasted about shooting down a Jap Zero with a bazooka while Uncle Katz called him a dumb jarhead, plain-assed too stupid to lie his way through a war story. A bazooka's back blast would have burned off his heels. The boys knew Wally was sticking out his jaw, bulldog-mean, one jowly blue-eyed Polack with biceps like canned hams. He looked that way when he got quiet after being loud. Every Christmas, he threatened to call John Anthony Dominic Donatelli in South Philadelphia.

He was right there with me, pointing out the shot—we roasted the bastard in his fuselage, he said.

Donatelli in the unions out there? Katz said.

The boys saw Wally pointing right in Katz's face, his finger thicker than lashing rope. I don't got to prove shit to you.

The old man always told them to shut up. It was his phone and nobody was calling Philadelphia and running up the bill.

Just relax and deal the cards, Wally, the old man said.

By 1972, all the local boys were home from Vietnam. John and Walt had served with the marines in Quang Tri, I Corps, and once ran into each other at the PX in Da Nang, where Jack was preordering a 1969 Mustang from a Ford rep. Stanley was 101st Airborne and got shot in the back coming out of a helicopter in the A Shau when the guy behind him tripped and his rifle went off—a dopey son of a bitch, he said, a goddamned dirt clod from Nebraska with big hands and this little-ass head.

The old man never did build a bigger table. He only brought down a folding table from upstairs, set it by the basement door, and gave the boys their own deck of cards. They tried telling the old men about Asia, the one-armed hookers, the guy who was court-martialed for sending an M60 home piece by piece and how he almost got the whole thing home but then his mother freaked out when the barrel came last and she brought the pieces to the Marine Corps recruiter and dumped them on his desk.

The old men got drunk too fast the Christmas before Saigon fell. Their eyes sank while they sorted their rummy hands with open mouths. The old man smoked his Camel thoughtfully and sipped his beer while Jack and Katz chewed cigars. Uncle Wally filled his highball glass, floating the ice cube, then set the bottle on the concrete floor. He looked at the table where Walt and his boys sat drinking and turning the cards like assembly-line workers. His eyes were twisted lifer-mean.

You know they had race riots at Camp Lejeune, he said. Just like goddamn Attica prison.

Uncle Wally stared sideways at the boys. The boys looked at the cinder-block walls.

What the hell did you do over there? he said.

John and Stanley were quiet and hated their old man with their eyes. Walt looked at his wrist when he didn't wear a watch.

That's all the fuck I want to know.

Uncle Wally was soused. The old man touched his shoulder to quiet him. He looked hard at his brother.

Play your hand, the old man said.

The boys sat there and took it. There was nothing Walt wanted to say, and he half-believed he'd done something wrong over there, even if he didn't know what. John and Stanley drifted away from Watega and took grunt jobs up north in Chicago and stopped even talking to each other. They didn't show up at Uncle Wally's funeral, after he had a heart attack cleaning the gutters. He rolled off the roof and fell facedown on the wet grass. It was a warm spring day, but cold in the shadows. The marine reserve unit in Glenview sent down an honor guard, and the old men took off their hats when taps blew. But his boys never came home.

The days of the first week were hot and windy and very white. The green cornstalks were turning yellow in the fields below the hilltop. He finished the concrete foundation within two days and built sawhorses from cast-off boards he found behind the house and sized the new two-by-fours for the frame with a handsaw. He then nailed together the wall frames in the rocky dirt with long sixteen-gauge nails.

One morning, he thought there was someone watching him from the pines. Shep looked at the trees and barked. He stayed the hammer to listen. The wind ran through the trees and the cones fell upon the ground, but when the wind lulled, he heard breaking sticks and then coughing. He took the nails from his mouth and stood with his hammer and pretended to hear something from the road by the river. The frames for the walls lay in the dirt behind where he'd raised them and he noticed cigarette butts among the rocks that were not his own. Shep paced and showed his yellow teeth and growled in low tones.

He got in his pickup with the dog and drove down the lane, where dry leaves crept in the bar ditch, then headed north along the gravel road. He turned on the blacktop for a moment and parked among the river trees and smoked a cigarette. He stepped out before the dog and climbed the wooded hillside, where he saw over his house from the south. Behind him was the river plain, covered with snarled goosegrass and wildflowers, and the green was fading from the tree leaves because the days were rainless and autumn was coming the way it would, all in a day. Shep's long hair dragged on the forest floor and he smelled mossy rocks, and cockleburss matted the fur around his paws. Walt walked until he found some deadfall, a lightning-struck hackberry, and lay prone behind it. He watched the house while the clouds blew across the sun, and sometimes the white heat dissolved them before they drifted away. To the west ran a creekbed along the side of the field, and beyond that two deer ran between the hedgerows. Shep lay beside him, his nose in the leaves, growling at an anthill.

"Shut up," Walt said.

The dog swallowed a whine and breathed through his long nose. Walt stroked his ears. Shep was very still, even though he smelled the deer in the wind.

He lay there, working snuff against his gum. He watched a long time, but nobody came. He held his chin in his hands. The sunlight fell on his neck. The sun was burning when Shep growled in his face. He sat up and took off his hat and looked. A kid was coming out of the pines with a skateboard, and even from this distance, Walt saw that his eyes popped like a lizard's.

The kid walked past the house and stopped at the concrete foundation. He wore baggy jeans cut off below the knees and a flannel shirt without sleeves. He dropped the skateboard on the foundation and looked up the hillside directly at Walt, then stepped on it and started doing tricks. He walked it. He jumped up and the skateboard twirled and he landed back square.

Walt waited until the kid was lost in his tricks, then skirted the woods behind the house, where the kid had left tracks in the pine needles. He walked up behind the ruined toolshed. Shep moved low behind him, then lay in the shadow the house made on the weeds. The kid was red-faced, crouched low on the skateboard, zigzagging on the foundation with clean movements that resembled close-order drill. Walt pitched a stone at the pile of two-by-fours, but the kid did not look up. He reached down and tapped Shep's hind quarters and the dog ran so fast at the kid that his head turned sideways.

Shep jumped and tackled the kid and straddled his chest,

barking. Spit flew into the sunlight. The kid flailed his arms and screamed. His legs were no bigger than fell sticks.

"You stalking me?" Walt said.

He was a kid about seventeen years old. Hair grew in patches on his thin face and bad acne covered what was left.

"Shit no, I ain't stalking you," the kid said.

"How come you been watching me?" Walt said.

"I ain't been watching you."

Walt stood with his arms folded across his chest and his boot heels sank in the sand. The kid squinted his eyes and tried turning away from Shep's teeth, but the dog followed all his movements and let go thin yelps.

"This dog's got some stinking-ass breath," the kid said.

"You waiting to rob me?" Walt said.

"No, goddammit. I just twirl my board on this concrete. There ain't no good places in Hall. Shitting cops chase you out of the church parking lot."

"You walk all the way out from Hall and wait for me to go to the lumberyard?"

The kid looked at him. Walt thought he scowled, but his face was made that way.

"What's your name?" Walt said.

"Call this dog off me."

"Tell me your name."

"Eight Ball."

Walt clapped his hands and Shep growled and snapped the air around the kid's red face.

"My goddamn name's Shirley Warren Haursperger."

"I can see why you go by Eight Ball," Walt said.

"Nobody calls me that. But I want them to."

"Where'd you come up with a name like that?" Walt said.

"I got it off MTV. It's my rapper's name. They got white boys do it just as good as blacks."

"Why the hell should I not call the cops on you?" Walt said.

The kid didn't answer. He lay looking past Shep at the yellow wind running in the oak leaves and at the shadows of the thin branches quaking across the rocky dirt. He looked up at Walt and tugged the long chain hooked between his belt and a leather trucker's wallet.

"Because I'm a white man," he said.

Walt spat and shook his head and looked at the hilltop where the coal mine had once been.

He sat that hot evening inside the screened porch so he could look up at the sky and smile about being on the hilltop. There were red storm clouds rising in the west and they soon turned black and covered the starlight. After awhile, it got very dark and the winds came up. The dog paced on the cracked porch boards and whined. The thunder clapped in the darkness, ahead of hard gusts that bent the sapling trees, and the rain came down sideways. He sat on the lawn chair until he was very wet. He stayed until his clothes were heavy with rain and then went inside and called the dog. He lay by the open door and listened to the rain and fought sleep for many hours because he wanted no other dream.

Not long after sunrise, Walt heard Shirley riding the skateboard upon the foundation from a handstand. He rose and lit the gas burner with a match and started coffee, then watched him through the bad glass. The kid had fashioned a ramp from cinder blocks and plywood sometime in the morning dark.

He poured his coffee and walked out on the porch in his

T-shirt. Shirley sped across the foundation and hit the ramp and spun in midair before falling into a sand pile. The dog was barking at him.

"You walk out here in the dark?" Walt said.

"I hitched half of it," Shirley said.

"Which half?"

"The first."

"That's kind of discouraging," Walt said.

Shirley went on standing. He looked up, confused.

"You still going to pay me twenty bucks for helping you today?"

Walt nodded and drank long from his coffee. The kid walked right up to him and he lit a cigarette. "You a gambler?" he said.

"No," Walt said.

"I'm trying to figure out why you moved out here. There isn't nothing but the gambling boat in Clinton. The rest's just hills and the river."

"I like the country," Walt said.

"I want to go to California and ride my skateboard. They got these places all set up for it. You can skate all day long and nobody says shit."

Shirley stopped smoking. Walt saw that his left earlobe was gnarled, as if dog-bitten. The kid was looking out at the country to the west, where the sun broke over the oaks that walled the Manteno River. Then he went on smoking.

"I might even get in the movies about skateboarding. Then I'm taking the money and going to ninja school in Japan."

Walt laughed.

"I ain't bullshitting you," Shirley said.

He stared bleakly at Walt and turned away. He stood and

pulled out a cheap butterfly knife and started working it. His eyes went cold. He affected stances with his skinny legs. He passed the knife behind his back, between his legs, and then threw it up in the air and caught it with his other hand. He smiled at Walt when he was done.

"I think I got the basic talent for ninja training," he said.

"Where'd you get that knife?"

"The carnival."

"Can you stick it in that tree," Walt said.

"This here's not a throwing knife. It's strictly for fighting up close."

Walt sat on the porch steps and slung the coffee grounds in the dirt. The sunlight glinted on the brown water between the river trees.

"You cut your ear with that thing?" he said.

"Some crazy nigger did this to me in the boys home over in Kewanee. I wasn't there for stealing."

"What'd you do?"

"Nothing. The nigger was crazy. He used to stand in your way and sing to himself."

"No. Why were you in the boys home?"

"I told the motherfucker he wasn't going to smack me no more. My mom even started taking his side against me."

"Your stepdad?"

Shirley nodded and played with the chain of his trucker's wallet.

"You stabbed him."

"He got scared I might."

"They don't put you away because somebody gets scared," Walt said.

"He used to drink vodka and lemonade. I'd piss in the lemonade and put it back in the refrigerator."

Walt leaned forward and shook his head.

"You pissed in his lemonade," he said.

"I used to watch him drink it."

They started work in the mornings when the sun broke over the Manteno River and glinted on the brown water. The kid held the frame upon the bolts formed in the concrete while Walt tightened the nuts; then they framed out the roof and hung it and walled the shed with Sheetrock. The days were hot and windy and the dust from the country hardened on their sweaty faces when they broke for water. The kid was a good helper, even though he had no talent for the work. The hammer wore the skin from his palms. His arms shook whenever he lifted more than a cigarette. He bent nails when he struck them. Walt told him that he could spend the nights on the hilltop, but he never did, just took his daily wage every afternoon and left with the skateboard over his shoulder, the chain from his trucker's wallet glinting sunlight. He walked along the dusty lane to skate the seven miles back to Hall, no bigger than the shadow of sticks. Walt was sure he would never return once he had sixty bucks in the wallet. He even decided he'd have to hire a man to help him insulate the shed, put up drywall, and run the electric, and he'd miss Shirley, because he never asked real questions, the way a man might. The kid always came back, standing by the work site in the morning dark and smoking cigarettes, his clothes always the same, but clean.

They ate lunch under the shade of the pines. The woodworking shop was done except for the roofing and some odd finish work inside. They ate roast beef sandwiches with thick slices of onion and potato chips, which the kid dipped in mustard, and drank bottled beer wet from the cooler ice. They leaned back on their elbows in the pine needles with their boots crossed before them, drinking quietly.

Shirley looked at Walt's forearm and then looked at him. His sunburn helped fade the acne.

"Where'd you get that tattoo? he said.

"Out in Oceanside, California," Walt said. "In the marines."

Shirley spat and sat looking. "They ripped you off," he said.

Walt shook his head and ground out his cigarette on a rock. "I got it a long time ago."

"I tried joining the marines last spring," Shirley said. "I even started the paperwork."

"You got scared," Walt said.

"A cat bit me when I was a kid and I got sick as hell."

"They'd of taken you in my time."

Shirley tilted his bony face to listen. His mouth hung open. "You were in Vietnam?" he said.

Walt nodded.

"You're lying out your ass," the kid said. "They're all young guys in Vietnam. I seen every movie about it."

"I was there thirty years ago."

"Vietnam wasn't thirty years ago. I saw a movie about it on HBO last week. They were all young and wanting to smoke pot."

Walt waved him away. He stood and swiped at the seat of his jeans with one hand and titled his hat back. Shirley had finished eating and sat tapping a Marlboro on the back of the pack.

"You cool?" Shirley said.

Walt looked down at the kid and saw his lips filthy from the dust. "Not looking at that roof we got to shingle," he said.

"No. You cool with making some money?"

"What do you know about making money?" Walt said.

Shirley shrugged and smiled at him. He drew on his cigarette and chewed on nothing. "You know anything about methamphetamines?" he said.

Walt looked off at the woods and then he looked at the kid. "How much?"

"Four hundred dollars a week. Maybe more."

"For what?" Walt said.

"Keeping your mouth shut when the wind smells like cat piss."

8

When Tom drove the old man into the woods, the dawn was less than an hour away and the old man was mad because he was serious about getting set in his ground blind two hours before sunrise. Tom shut down the truck and shook his head while the old man drew on his cigarette so hard that his cheeks caved. Tom blew cold and looked at him. His skin was like wet paper. The blue veins swelled in his forehead.

"The deer will smell us coming into the woods," the old man said. "You won't even see a stray spiker."

Tom looked off at the hill that rose behind the bare trees, the place where someone had started a house twenty years ago and got no further than the footings. He waited for the old man to make a crack about the guy losing everything in a carpet business.

"You wear your ass for a hat in the army, too?" the old man said.

"Maybe we can hire some Mexicans to take you out next weekend," Tom said.

"At least they'll answer the bell in the morning."

Tom got out, went to the back of the truck, and took down the wheelbarrow with the folding chair welded into the bucket. The old man had made it five years ago. He couldn't walk these woods anymore, so whoever took him hunting wheeled him over the frozen mud through the scrub oaks to his blind. Tom remembered when he was a boy how he'd coughed and broken sticks so the old man would not take him hunting. It was Teddy the old man wanted with him, the boy who couldn't remember his last name but had already shot three bucks by his tenth birthday.

The old man leaned his shotgun against the truck when Tom came with the wheelbarrow. Some blackbirds flew out of the field and circled the bare trees. Tom put the step stool down and the old man used his shoulder for a handhold. He stepped up for the wheelbarrow and his knee buckled. He fell against Tom and straightened himself, then spat and kicked weakly at the stool.

"What's the matter?" Tom said.

"You build something to last and then you watch it get pissed away."

The old man sat down and laid the shotgun across his knees. His jeans hung slack around his gaunt hips.

"You got to set them up with something good," he said.

Tom scratched the mud with his boot. He was quiet. The old man looked off at the darkness through the woven branches.

"You know them buildings in New York aren't like Pearl Harbor," he said. "There's nothing the same about what's coming after."

Tom waited for the old man to say more, but he didn't. He wheeled him past the creek, where the ice was jagged along the bank, and went through a small meadow of goosegrass, and the squirrels perched in the trees looked at them. The old man slouched loosely in the chair. The wheel left a faint rut in the frozen mud.

The old man looked at Tom when they came to his blind between two hickory trees. He loaded the shotgun and laid it across his thighs. He sat erect and scanned the woods. The hunt had started and Tom better not break a stick with his boot when he walked off. The old man listened and counted them popping and would tell him about it later.

Tom walked off along the creek. Ahead was the Watega River, high from the November rains and flowing between the trees without visible movement. He had become a soldier because he wanted to be the old man and not a cuckolded shopkeeper like his father. The Medal of Honor encased in glass above the TV set. Men knowing that he'd jumped into Normandy and single-handedly silenced a German .88 gun with two hand grenades and an M1 carbine, killing eleven. The old man never talked about it. He sat at bars and let other men tell each other the story. Tom wanted that the most. The guys whispering how the old man got drunk on a hunting trip and thought he was in the hedgerows, the hate welling up in his eyes like dark ice. Tom loved walking into diners with the old man and watching the coffee counter go silent while they all rose to shake his hand and wonder how this Polack plumber had made a million dollars digging sewer lines.

His tree stand was a sheet of plywood squared over two branches in a hickory. Tom left his shotgun unloaded and leaned it against an oak and sat down on the cold leaves. He would seem like a hunter only to men who had never hunted. He stared at the flooded river and hoped the old man took his shot early.

He heard birds overhead from the fields out east. It was too dark to see them.

The last time Tom saw Uncle Walt before the Vietnam trip was a Sunday morning five years ago, when they drove to the hospital in Joliet, where the old man was recovering from hip-replacement surgery. He'd broken it falling out of a tree stand, and Tom came home on Christmas leave to see him. A hard wind had knocked him out of the oak like a crooked stick. That was how Uncle Walt put it. They hadn't seen a deer.

The bar ditches along Route 50 overflowed from the early-morning rains and brown water flooded the long stretches of road. Uncle Walt ignored the hazard triangles left by the county. The water came past his wheel wells and the truck engine faded but never died. His eyes were bloody from a hangover and he did not notice the blinking alternator light or the muddy water pooling on the floormats. He squeezed the steering wheel to keep his hands from shaking. He was crazy after catching his third wife, Sherry, giving a blow job to Jeff Brosseau, some kid just home from the navy.

Uncle Walt dragged on his Marlboro and pitched it out the window. There were many hedge trees between the fields and the wind blew the wet leaves across the bar ditch. He opened a sales folder from the Harley-Davidson store on the bench seat between them. A blonde in a leather bikini lay over a sky blue motorcycle with glinting chrome. Her ankles were raised and crossed. He pointed at the picture and drove.

See this Heritage Soft Tail, he said. You got to order it a year out.

You're not buying one, Tom said.

A Harley ain't like a car or a boat. It holds its value. This motorcycle is a real sound investment. Like a treasury bond.

Who told you that? Tom said.

The guy at Mason's Harley-Davidson," Walt said. "Next year, I could sell it for two thousand more than I paid.

Tom said nothing. Walt's eyes shifted between the flooded road and the picture.

I don't give a shit what the old man thinks, he said.

When you going to put the money down? Tom said.

His uncle looked at him. Sweat slid along the wrinkles creased into his face.

I need about seven grand to get things started, Walt said.

The Harley?

I know how I could turn your seven grand into twenty before you sign back in off leave.

Tom looked at Walt and his red eye whites. The rain slanted into the windshield and made hard sounds. Walt smiled and the lines in his face disappeared into his beard.

Can you get me that much by tomorrow morning? he said.

I don't mess with dope, Tom said.

There's this kid down at Rat's, Walt said. He's shit-scared of me. I asked him what he thought I'd do if he ever ripped me off. You know what he said?

Tom shook his head and dragged on his cigarette.

That I'd kill him, Walt said. Everything's safe. The little fucker will play it straight.

Tom was quiet for a minute.

I'm a soldier, he said.

The road went straight toward Joliet through the low fields and they drove in silence. Tom figured they'd put the old man off until tomorrow if Walt found a bar open this early on a Sunday.

Tom knew Uncle Walt was not the guy in Vietnam who talked about going home to drive the wheels of a 1969 GTO convertible. He never put on the barracks show where he wiggled his tongue at a Playboy *centerfold. The old man had convinced him early he could do nothing but unclog toilets on service calls. The real shit-talker was Hill the heartbreaker, Hill the life-taker, or sometimes just Hill the blue-eyed country boy who talked fast and looked good in sunglasses. The way Walt talked, Irvin Hill was the James Bond of Kentucky and cooler than Steve McQueen in* The Great Escape. *Hill somehow got the money to drive away in a 1969 GTO the minute he got stateside. He'd preordered the car at the PX in Da Nang and had it waiting in San Diego. He was slick enough to miss the fight in Con Thien by a day, and flew off smiling from Dong Ha like a cat who sees bad things ten seconds before they happen. Walt was sure life had been nothing but blue skies and California coastline for Irvin Hill. He only drove to drive, Walt said, and banged two women prettier than Ali McGraw before lunchtime. Tom's uncle judged his life these thirty-five years against how he imagined things had turned out for Hill.*

Walt blew smoke through his nose and pointed at the motorcycle.

I should have it by May, he said. Then I'm taking off to look up old Hill.

You even know how to find this guy? Tom said.

It ain't about finding anything, he said. It's about the looking.

The countryside changed after they passed the Otto Crossroads. The river angled off from them, the woods and the railroad tracks were gone from the roadside, and, quite suddenly, there was nothing but the acres of ruined cornfields. Tom saw the ridge of pines overlooking the river bend where Uncle Walt had shot Teddy. The needles were green against the gray overcast. Walt had never told Tom about that morning, but it was something there, like the field roads of Watega County. Uncle Walt drove without words while the country appeared with a quiet brutality. The corn was harvested and the land ran flat and straight toward the horizon. Walt held the wheel tightly and stared out at the cut cornstalks twisted in the mud, the sagging barbed wire strung between the fence posts, the sallow skies that ran far beyond the curve of the earth. Tom looked with him. It was too much space to contemplate all at once.

They didn't see the old man until that evening. Walt closed the sales folder and drove around the country until bars opened. There was the sportsmen's club near the river bend where the Watega turned north into the Illinois. They would have a fire going—Walt was sure of it—and free meatballs warmed by Sterno. They'd grab a table by the fireplace and drink Jack Daniel's with beer chasers and watch the brown river spool past. Walt's mood lightened just thinking about it. He drove very fast along the flooded roads, before the club filled with deer hunters in their Day-Glo vests and they took all the tables and forced Walt and Tom to sit along the bar with the old men who spat on the floor.

The old man took his shot around noon and missed. Tom heard it and grabbed the shotgun from against the tree and headed for his blind. It was cold walking through the woods, but the sun was breaking through the clouds and the light felt warm on his face. The old man was already unloaded when he got there, the shotgun broken and lying across his knees. His face seemed carved from soap. He put a cigarette in his mouth but couldn't spark the match, and he threw it all in the weeds. Tom saw the hoof tracks in the mud and the gored hickory bark where the slug had hit.

"That buck came from your way," the old man said.

"No."

"I know what the hell I saw. He came from the river."

The buck had run past Tom and skirted the river trees. The deer moved powerfully and shook the wood vine from his ten points. These were the buck's woods and he searched the scrub trees for stray fawns. Tom thought about shooting high and scaring the buck back toward the riverbank, but he knew the old man was already too cold for setting a decent shot, his fingers numb, his mind focused on the pain in his hip. Tom wanted the old man to shoot and miss.

"I saw a couple spikers after dawn," Tom said.

"You might of dreamed two spikers. But you didn't see shit."

Tom wheeled him out of the blind and headed for the truck, hoping the cold had caused his arthritic hip to flare up enough to spoil tomorrow's hunt. The old man kept sticking his hand beneath his rump and lifting, as if that would do something.

The old man drove home and took sharp turns in the road that went through the forest. He went up a hill that rose over the fields, then stopped and pulled off by the bar ditch. The road was lined with trees on both sides and through the right row Tom saw the fields, the furrow lines muddy, flooded, and brown. The old man left the engine running for the heat. The wind gusted hard and sticks went spinning off the roadside trees, taking flight as if birds.

"We waiting out the wind?" Tom said.

"I've strung wire fence in worse weather than this."

"You ever seen a cow blown over?" Tom said.

"I've seen plow horses pushed backward. But a cow will lay down before it falls over."

"You sure about that?"

"What the hell do you know about horses and cows?"

The old man looked at him and then looked where the sun left cloud shadows on the fields. The shadow line ran jagged across the road. His hand trembled when he let go of the wheel. Tom looked away while sticks hit the truck and broke. The old man reached in his coat pocket and came out with a dirty envelope and dropped it on the bench seat. He grabbed the wheel to stay his hand. Tom saw where he'd held the envelope many afternoons and just thought. He cracked the window to smoke, but the old man shook his head before he lit the cigarette.

"I want you to listen," he said.

"I can smoke and do that," Tom said.

"Put the goddamned cigarettes away."

The old man was looking out at the country in the west, where sunlight broke the cloud seams and glinted upon the brown river. The cab turned very cold from the cracked window.

"There's fifteen grand in there," he said. "Give Jimmy Ruell five and you boys go find Walt."

"He's got the bar to run," Tom said.

"When Red Ruell retires, he's selling Jarhead's to the highest bidder. Don't shit yourself. A kid like Jimmy Ruell couldn't save five grand in a lifetime."

The old man waved Tom quiet before he could speak. Then he grabbed the wheel again to stay his hand. The veins beneath his knuckles were ropy.

"You go get your uncle," he said. "I know he's in Hall County. People are talking."

The old man pushed the envelope against Tom's leg and started the truck. They drove down into the windy valley.

Tom Jane and Jimmy Ruell headed out 113 along the river like they had as boys. Jimmy drove without headlights and they saw deer in the starlight, and in the starlight the deer were white as the moon and as distant. The bucks kept watch with glowing eyes while the does and the fawns dug into the furrow lines for corn. The pickup scared the deer and they broke in pairs and loped across the gored earth until neither man could see them anymore.

They parked east of Warner Bridge and built a fire from driftwood. The night was clear and without wind and they blew cold in the firelight while the sparks popped into the river. They could see headlights strafing through the trees on the far bank a long time before hearing the cars. Jimmy opened a fifth of Jim Beam and they both took swigs and Tom capped the bottle and set it outside the firelight.

"We'll split the money even, Ruell," Tom said. "All you got to do is come along."

Jimmy took the whiskey bottle from the dark and sat holding it by the neck.

"You get the money when you bring him back?"

"I got it now."

"Your grandpa just don't give money away."

Tom didn't answer for a while. Then he said, "No, he don't."

"He just wants to rub Walt's face in it all until he's too dead inside to care."

"He might be that dead now," Tom said.

"It's why he left."

"You got other plans?" Tom said.

Jimmy uncapped the bottle and drank long. Tom looked at him and threw his cigarette in the fire.

"You got more reason to leave than me," Jimmy said.

"No, I don't."

"Most of us come back eight years ago," Jimmy said. "Me and O'Brien bought motorcycles and drove out to California and did the whole thing. We tried being pissed-off Gulf War vets, but after a year, we decided we'd watched too many movies."

"You think your old man's going to die tomorrow and leave you that bar?"

Jimmy said nothing.

"Well, he's not," Tom said.

"I don't need you to tell me that."

"Then what you staying around here for? We could take the money and go to Vietnam."

"What we going to do there, Jane? Work odd jobs?"

"Teach English in Saigon. Ten grand's a lot of money there."

Jimmy shook his head.

"I talked to some Australians. All you got to be is a native speaker."

"You might know about being a soldier," Jimmy said. "But you know nothing about being a civilian. People build lives out here."

"And Lisa's coming back tomorrow. I bet she'll want you to knock her up. First thing."

Jimmy shook a cigarette from the pack on the ground and put it in his mouth and tried striking a match. Tom held up a burning stick and Jimmy lit it that way. His face glowed orange like the bottom of the fire.

"At least you had the Gulf War," Tom said.

"It was the biggest letdown of my life."

"But I missed it."

"You'd think that volunteering for the Rangers would have gotten you there first."

"Some of us had to be in reserve."

"For other things."

"Sure," Tom said. "For other things."

"Them Iraqis were too pathetic to fight. Some of them were bleeding from the ears after six weeks of being bombed. They just come up with their hands over their heads and started blathering and kissing our boots."

"You never wanted to fight them?"

"I did before I saw them. I even wanted you there with me. But after seeing them, it would have been like kicking a stray dog. There was this sergeant who started slapping them around because he could. It wasn't even dignified."

"But at least you got in it."

"They even gave me the Bronze Star and I don't know what I did for it. The CO threatened me with an Article Fifteen if I didn't take it. You know how they are about that shit."

Tom tipped the bottle up and drank from it, then lowered it, screwed the cap back on, and set the bottle on the ground.

"I know how they are about that shit," he said.

9

The *Hall County Republican* ran an editorial cartoon of Dwight's head on the muscled body of Rambo while he shot down pigs with a belt-fed machine gun. The caption simply read *"Holding the line."* Women wrote letters to the paper, blaming him for missing cats, road-killed deer, dogs that limped home with broken legs, a bad die-up of minnows in Rock Creek. Verda Soucie from Cherry wrote that her daughter had been crying every day since hog killings and hiding under blankets with Lucy, their dog, afraid that he'd kill her if she went outside, and the kid lay in dog shit for a week. Somebody made ten white crosses and put them on the roadside near the field where he'd shot the pigs. People left flowers. They sent canned hams to the Sheriff's Department. The Imperial Diner served toasted peek and cheese at lunchtime, peek and beans for supper. Sheriff Tim Bertrand told Dwight he wanted to fire him, send him out with bad paper, but Hennepin Steel had gotten a government contract, adding two hundred jobs, and the applicant pool in Hall County couldn't pass the drug screening. Dwight was damned lucky. A real skate, the sheriff said. "You're going to be the new secretary until people stop laughing," Bertrand told Dwight.

Dwight was typing at the desk by the shotgun rack when Les Styck walked inside with his smart grin. He was a fat farmer who didn't have a neck and he panted from having climbed the courthouse steps in the heat. Jerry Bowman had his .45 in pieces on the reception counter, swabbing off the oiled carbon with Q-Tips, and every few minutes he wondered out loud about how Dwight liked being a chair-bound commando these last weeks. The windows were open and the glass glowed white from the sunlight and the ceiling fan kept blowing Dwight's papers on the floor. Les took off his hat but never wiped the sweat from his forehead. He smiled at Bowman and rolled his eyes.

"Hey, Peek," he said. "How come you didn't let at least one little piggy go all the way home?"

"This here's a stone-cold killer," Bowman said.

"A regular life-taker and heartbreaker," Styck said.

"Hey, commando," Bowman said. "You having any problems with post-traumatic stress disorder?"

Dwight typed the accident report. Yesterday, the teenagers who rode skateboards in the Lutheran church parking lot had made their noses into pig snouts when he drove past. The other deputies taped bacon packages to his locker door. He took the jokes and waited for the topic to disappear from barrooms and diner counters the way the birds did every November.

Les Styck dripped sweat on the counter. Gray hair snarled from his ears. He was the richest farmer in Hall County, but you wouldn't know it, ragged overalls, a salt-rimed Dekalb Seed Company hat. He owned nearly a thousand acres of bottomland and employed twenty Mexicans, putting them up in a cinder-block barracks he'd built near the river. They'd get drunk and start fighting, and Les always had a story about it: "Them boys from Sonora are the worst. They'll pull knives when they get to losing."

Jerry Bowman picked up the barrel of his .45 and looked through it.

"Shit, Les," he said. "Somebody must have told you about dropping a quarter in here to get you up them stairs. You were assholes and elbows. I saw you."

Les gestured out the window with his double chin.

"Somebody's siphoning off my ammonia fertilizer," he said. "They hit two tanks last night. I found an intertube all eaten to shit down by the creek. Like the son of a bitch thought it'd hold anhydrous ammonia."

"You sure them Mexicans ain't sniffing it when the Parkway Inn cuts them off?" Bowman said. "You had some last year who'd drink Windex."

"It'd collapse your lungs. Just like getting emphysema and dying from it all in a minute."

"Peek will take your complaint," Bowman said. "Bertrand's got him doing that real regular. Ain't that right, Peek? What'd Tim tell you?"

Dwight forced a grin and hit the return on the typewriter. The bell rung.

"Typing will take the itch out of my trigger finger," he said.

"I told Tim you can't change a natural-born killer," Bowman said.

"Like teaching a pig to dance," Les said.

"Yessir."

He waddled back to the desk and sat down, breathing hard through his nose. He looked at Dwight and then at Jerry.

"You smell bacon?" he said.

Dwight knew why people were stealing ammonia fertilizer.

They used it for cooking methamphetamine because it boiled down faster. They sprayed it over shoplifted Sudafed, lithium strips from D batteries, ether extracted from starting fluid, and five hours later there was enough crank to keep twenty-five tweakers speeding for a month. "White-trash cocaine," they called it, made in the woods and fields like moonshine because the chemicals smelled worse than cat litter, and all the ingredients came from Wal-Mart. Dwight knew it before they found the first ammonia-burned kid walking along the ditch on 166, his bugged eyes on the ground ahead, the skin scorched from his palms, or when Jim Farrell saw another kid lying along the corn furrows, gasping like a drowned man, his left lung collapsed from the fumes. Dwight kept his mouth shut because this was for Tim Bertrand to figure out. When two teenagers had their faces burned off after a tank of stolen fertilizer exploded in their trunk, freezing their skin to the seats of their Camaro, the sheriff still didn't know why they were doing it. They'd siphoned the gas into a propane grille tank, and the anhydrous ammonia ate away the brass fittings. The car sat for three days outside the county garage, the doors and trunk open to air it out. Two days later, the smell made Jack Soucie, the tow-truck driver, puke bile on the tool bench.

Dwight lay flat in the dry furrowed dirt of the cornfield, his chin on the shotgun metal, and overhead the night wind blew the tassels of the cornstalks. The field was flat where he lay, but before him the ground sloped and he could see the cylindrical fertilizer tank, white in the summer moonlight. There were tractor ruts behind the tank and beyond it a creekbed, and looking farther down the ruts, he could see a ruined corncrib and the dry rocks of the bed where the creek turned and headed upcountry.

For three nights, he waited on his belly in the field dust. They would come and hit this tank. He was sure of it. There were no farmhouses near, and the man who tended these fields had left his unused fertilizer tanks from the spring right where he'd needed them next May when he infused the anhydrous ammonia into the brown earth. The thieves were probably lazy and would siphon the leftovers from the tank and then head along the rocky creekbed past the hedgerows, then through the overgrown field, planted with sorghum for quail hunting, and walk for the river, where the hickory trees grew around the dark of the swamp, a hike of less than two miles. There, they would cook their meth, needing to be far from houses and roads because the smell was strong, though Dwight had never smelled it. He only read these things on the Internet, usually serial news stories from small towns in Kansas or Tennessee, titled "Meth: Nightmare in the Heartland." The articles told him to look for subtle clues, tire tracks on dirt roads, clusters of trash in the woods, coffee filters, aerosol cans, and the abandoned coolers used to carry the fertilizer. He spent his weekends searching the pine hills in the east end of the county, the brackish thickets along the river flats west of Powell's Bridge, but he found nothing. He even walked around the Wal-Mart in Dixon, waiting for kids to buy cold medicine, or a cartful of D batteries, and he planned to tail them off into the country, but the kids were only looking at the cheap skateboards and baggy shorts, calling one another "dog."

When they came, he would be ready: dark in his night-stalker fatigues, camouflage stick dulling his face and hands, applied the way the U.S. Army Ranger manual instructed, his shotgun loaded with buckshot, and a knife scabbard attached with Velcro to his right ankle. He would break the whole ring, maybe get a conspiracy charge against ten, and assist the DEA in mopping up the leftover perpetrators. A sting like this would make him, and the DEA would send the letter to his trailer in the woods, asking him to join, not telling him he did not meet their basic qualifications. He'd never be Peek again. Nobody would know a thing about him passing out towels in high school. He'd be a true force, a fed, probably hunting narcoterrorists in Colombia, night patrols through the rain forests with automatic weapons, attack helicopters waiting for his orders to let loose with 30-mm cannons.

The wind was up over the hill. He thought about the time when he'd guarded the gold for class rings in Peoria, working with grim-faced retired guys who did word finds with ballpoints, dreamless men like his father, who spent thirty years on nights at the Caterpillar factory. They sat in chairs for ten bucks an hour and listened to talk radio and never talked. Dwight was a ghost. He had Tuesday and Wednesday nights off, and he went to a strip joint called Big Al's by the Illinois River, where tour buses ferrying farmers idled at the curb. He thought this red-haired dancer named Melody really liked him. Her hair was teased and her breasts were hard like inflated footballs. When it was slow, she gave him lap dances for ten bucks instead of twenty. She smiled and shook and looked right in his eyes. He wanted to take her to Red Lobster, maybe the Olive Garden. It would set him back, but she was worth someplace nice. He dreamed of picnics by the river, Christmas shopping out at the mall, bringing the old guys guarding the gold the cookies she baked him. One night, she gave him a real dance, straddling his thighs, working her breasts so close to his face, they brushed his cheeks. She smiled, blew kisses. Then he touched her waist and she went cold and stepped backward, cursing him. She called the bouncers, fat guys with big arms. He waited outside by her red Camaro to say he was sorry and to ask her to dinner, but the bouncers chased him off with baseball bats.

Two nights later, the kid came after the rain, a light summer rain, wetting the cornstalks, so the moonlight streaked the leaves. He was a gaunt wreck, walking up out of the dark, wearing sneakers gathered shut with duct tape. Every two steps, he stopped and looked, like a squirrel on a tree trunk, then sneezed and hacked phlegm gouts. He wore leather gloves in the heat and carried a small tank and a metal conduit.

He stopped before the fertilizer tank and dropped his gear. He sniffed, spat, then swallowed. He wiped his nose with a swipe from his sweaty arm. The night turned white from the silent lightning. The sour reek of the kid was everywhere and the darkness did not smell like the rain anymore. Dwight could hear the kid's troubled breathing, deep wet sounds, while he rigged the conduit between the fertilizer tank and the smaller one he'd brought and raised a bandanna around his nose and mouth. He was not well. When he turned the valves, the lightning flared and startled him, so that his neck spun too far the wrong way, and soon the sour smell of him was gone like the scents of rain. The ammonia sucked the air from the field. Dwight's eyes bleared. He lost his breath. The kid went on siphoning, his cough a rattle.

The kid was done within five minutes. After he closed the valves, he threw the conduit off into the yellow cornstalks. He went walking along the tire ruts that separated the fields, lugging the tank with two hands, his skinny arms bent at the elbow. He was a tall kid, uncomfortable with his height. Dwight let him go until he was near the hedgerows and then followed him, staying inside the rowed cornstalks. He walked with the shotgun pointed skyward.

The kid's lanky figure receded into the woods ahead. He walked on, then stopped and set down the tank and rested his arms. He waved them around until he fell into a coughing fit. Dwight waited in the trees until the kid started moving again and entered the woods to the left of him through some prairie grass. The burned-looking hickories twisted from the ground, misshapen by lightning strikes, and the branches hung like broken arms.

Dwight stayed to the kid's left and moved only when he did. He could smell the stagnant water and the rank swamp mud that bottomed the thicket. The kid breathed hard and slowed his pace, looking in all directions. Then a flashlight beam shot straight up from the creekbed that fed the river from the fields. It strobed the branches. Dwight knelt down in the scrub. The kid stumbled toward the light and the tank pulled both his arms straight.

When Dwight moved toward the creekbed, he walked in a crouch and knelt every five steps. He kept the shotgun shouldered, his eye down the short barrel, a hand on the wooden pump. Suddenly, a blue glow rose above the creekbed and he smelled propane. He stopped behind a berm and crawled along it. Sweat stung the corners of his eyes. Fire ants bit his cheeks. He took the pain, holding his breath. He crawled until the creekbed made a short S and then turned toward the riverbank. He tried to peer down into it, but the berm and the slanted weeds were too high, so he kept moving on his stomach. He found an opening before the canebrake and looked down. There was the blue flame, and he saw blurry figures. He waited, making sure the shadows were not people, and decided there were only two.

They stood there with a stove burning. There were two plastic buckets and three glass coffeepots on the rocks. The kid coughed into a balled fist while a fat guy held a Ziploc bag full of cash to the blue light. He turned it around, then opened it and looked inside. Dwight could not see his face, but his hair was long, holding the blue light.

"You son of a bitch," the guy said. "This of better not be a goddamned nigger wad, ones curled inside the twenties."

"It ain't," said the kid.

The fat guy was trying to make his laugh sound crazy. His waist fat bounced against his dark T-shirt. He wanted to scare the kid that way.

"I said it ain't."

The kid was wild-looking and out of breath. He stared at the fat guy and waited.

"How do I know you didn't pay yourself already?" the guy said.

"Shit."

The fat man walked to the ammonia tank, and when the kid didn't move, he hit him on the side of his head and the kid slumped back and fell against the berm. Dwight saw there were too many chemicals, so he decided to use his .45 with the laser sight because the buckshot might hit something. The fat man went past the kid and stood staring down at the tank the boy'd lugged across the fields.

"What did you use to siphon it?"

"A metal pipe."

"You wear gloves."

"No."

"You dumb shit. You'd burn off your hands for crank."

When the fat man dug into the bag to give the kid a bill, Dwight raised the pistol, leveled it, and tagged the fat guy's chest with the laser site.

"Police," Dwight said. He didn't recognize his own voice.

The guy looked at the red dot and then at Dwight, who was in a crouch like they'd taught him to do at the Academy. The man's face was a sweaty clot of whiskered acne. He dropped the money and reached for his pocket. The kid coughed wildly and backed into the sandy berm. Dwight pulled the trigger before thumbing off the safety. He saw the kid's wet eyes, quaking like limbs in the wind, then squeezed again.

When the pistol fired, the round hit the guy where the red dot had glowed. His chest exploded and slathered the kid with gore and his hat flew into the low tree branches and his eye whites bulged as if this were no more than a fevered dream. He fell sideways, landing on the stove and snuffing out the blue flame. His gut spilled from his T-shirt and the snap of his jeans was undone.

Dwight turned and tagged the kid, who was gagging from the raw propane. He trembled, his thin body seeming to be assembled from cornstalks. Dwight left the red dot on his chest and smiled, feeling giddy. *I killed a man and they can't touch me for it. Worst thing you can do, and I get to go home and eat frozen pizza like I'd just painted cars for eight hours.*

He walked forward with one eye on the dead fat man. He

tried frowning, but he couldn't move his lips. He looked at the money, the stacks of twenties shoved inside the freezer bag, thick as T-bone steaks. Six or seven grand, he guessed. He looked at the kid, who tried breathing past the phlegm clotted in his throat, then turned off the stove. He was a man above things now. He had bigger ideas, all within seconds, his world changing the way a summer storm rises up into blue skies and slaughters the cornfields with hail.

"What's your name?"

The kid said nothing. Dwight lifted the dot so it stuck to his forehead.

"Shirley Haursperger," the kid said.

"You know who I am?"

"You shot up the pigs."

"How'd you like half this money?" Dwight said.

The kid looked at the dead guy. His jeans were coming unzipped, his genitals spilling out with hair and fat. The kid nodded.

"You know how to make meth?" Dwight said.

"Better than this fat fucker."

"You sell it for him?"

The kid looked at him with roily eyes.

"I want half of everything. At night, I'm the only law for two hundred square miles of Hall County. I don't want to know where you sell it."

The kid nodded. "I bet that was some fun shit," he said. "Just blowing them hogs away."

Dwight lowered the pistol and thumbed on the safety. He pointed to the dead guy. The blood pooled in the stove, the flow stanched by dust.

"He with anybody?"

"He's from Peoria. He works all alone. I met him on the computer."

Dwight smiled. Things were different now.

10

Walt stood with the dog in the big door of the woodworking shop, his throat dry and burning all the way down. The wind came from the pine trees that stood before the ridge, then quit. Blackbirds flew off the hilltop without calls. The kid was hidden away in the thickets, cooking the meth, and Walt had never even seen him enter the woods. The smell appeared the way hard rains did, a heavy, windless downpour of ammonia, so thick that Walt felt like he could grab a handful from the autumn light and throw it against a tree. His eyes collapsed and the dog ran inside the shop and barked at the wall. Walt wiped his face with a wet rag and pulled down the door.

Already the shop stank from the meth. He put a bandanna over his nose and mouth and started up the table saw. He'd bought it with the first four hundred dollars the kid gave him, fives and tens stuffed into an envelope, sweaty from the kid riding his skateboard out here on bony legs, the portraits of Lincoln and Hamilton defaced with Hitler mustaches, devil's horns, a joint burning between their pursed lips. He mitered and beveled old two-by-fours. He made joints, then cut small boards from pine logs. He dreamed of rain, cold autumn lightning cracking into the cut cornfields that surrounded the hilltop on every side. He pushed the wood against the saw blade and wished it were chilly enough to see his breath. He worked an hour, filling the cement floor with sawdust, then stopped and watched the blade. He drew his shirt over the bandanna. He put his hand over that. His eyes ran, the tears like oil.

The cyclo driver followed him from the hotel and over the Truong Tien bridge, where below tugs pulled empty barges by towline along the Perfume River. Tommy was off with Tuyen from the bar, riding around Hue behind her on a Suzuki motorscooter, off beyond the old city to the pine hills with their calm lakes and moss-covered pagodas. Charlie's daughter, and she just wants to sing American radio songs, he thought. Walt could have been behind her on the scooter, smelling her tiny neck, his chest all over her back, but he'd given her to Tommy. That was the only reason.

The driver was a lean-hipped man in worn brown pants and had a mustache curled over his lip. The chain on his cyclo slipped every fourth rotation. Scooters and bicycles sped ahead of a small truck with a life-size picture of Ho Chi Minh, driven by a young woman with gloves that covered her arms against the sun. Vietnamese flags lined the bridge and Walt had seen old men hanging them outside the shops on Le Loi Street when the driver first started after him. He'd grinned at Walt and pointed to the cyclo chair.

You want ride, he said. Five dollar. Old city.

Maybe later, Walt said.

I here until later.

The truck passed over the bridge and played martial music and headed toward Le Loi Street and the new hotels built by the

French. Twenty old men in white uniforms followed on motor scooters. The driver pedaled five feet behind him, his pants dirty around his thin haunches. He wore sandals without heel straps and his feet were white from the dust. Walt looked at Ho Chi Minh and his white beard, the old guy stroking the heads of children who offered flowers and rice. Today was the twenty-sixth anniversary of Hue's liberation and Walt was the only person watching the parade. The Vietnamese all moved as unsmiling as cats, the sun-wrinkled women carrying baskets of mangoes suspended from a pole, the young men with cigarettes thrusting from their mouths while pulling handcarts of watermelons, the girls with their faces wrapped against the dust.

Two more cyclo drivers came upon Walt from the left. They'd been boys a few years ago. The driver yelled in Vietnamese, telling them to fuck off with his fingers, waving his sleeved arm until they pedaled away. At the traffic light, Walt saw the Thoung Tu Gate of the Citadel, where bullet holes gored the stone walls, relics from the battle Hill and he had missed by hours the day the artillery rounds chased their C-130 down the runway at Dong Ha, the morning they headed back home, thinking only of brand-new GTOs. The driver pulled up beside Walt and rolled up his sleeve. His arm was long and brown, with a fading tattoo below his shoulder. He pointed at the USMC globe and anchor on Walt's forearm.

We the same, he said.

Walt was wrung with sweat. The Vietnamese was dry. He couldn't make out the guy's tattoo.

Saigon marine. The best. I sergeant.

He stuck out a hand for Walt to shake and Walt did out of reflex. The Vietnamese smiled toughly where he sat on the cyclo seat. The air was filled with scooter horns.

You ride, marine? the Vietnamese said.

Walt looked up the street. Two other cyclo drivers were waiting for him. An old woman was hobbling up behind him with an empty rice basket. Walt reached in his pocket and gave the guy a five-dollar bill. He climbed down into the cyclo seat and it sank. The man laughed, pointing at his sweaty beer gut.

We no more marine, he said. We papa-sanh now.

Thirty-three years, Walt thought.

You wake up, old man, the Vietnamese said. One day.

The man pedaled the cyclo. It could have been empty. Walt felt like he was riding on the hood of a car through Chicago traffic. The driver stayed close to the curb and they went along the old city walls and crossed a stagnant moat where two boys stood pissing. He saw old M60 tanks parked in a row, a 175-mm howitzer, the hull of a Huey helicopter. Schoolkids in blue uniforms with red bandannas crawled on ruins. They played a game with sticks and laughed, and a few screamed hello at Walt. He waved back and looked at his tourist map. It was the War Relics Museum.

That night, he drank beer with the cyclo driver in a bar across the street from the hotel. He wondered why the man put his empty cans beneath the table. When Tinh became drunk, his face went all sideways. They had twenty words of English between them, and after four beers, Walt found it difficult compressing his questions into the set. After a while, Tinh just used a stock answer. No problem, he'd say, after Walt asked him what had happened to Hue after March 1975, or how the Communists had treated the old ARVN soldiers. Soon, Walt only smoked and smiled and bought more rounds. But the Tiger beer tasted better than thirty-three years ago. They didn't use formaldehyde anymore to speed the fermentation, and the Tiger looked calmer on the label. It wasn't jumping off the can with crazy eyes, claws out. This would scare a kid, Hill once said. Fill his pants with runny shit. The beer almost tasted like the Chicago microbrew Red Ruell tried selling for three bucks a bottle. When Walt stood to head for the Huong Giang Hotel, he swayed and staggered, knocking over the empty cans. The bartender looked at him from the door, shaking his head. Tinh reached over and grabbed his arm and smiled in a serious way. You have good time in Vietnam, he said. But not too good time. You know?

He stood outside the bar on Le Loi Street and watched the green neon blink of the Huda beer billboard across the river. The clouds were low, hammered close to the pine hills west of Hue, and a small rain caught the neon green and it seethed and ran through the darkness as a hundred scooter lights crossed the bridge away from the old city. The Vietnamese sat on plastic stools before shops lit by dim white bulbs, a light that hardly cast their shadows down upon the sidewalks, and stared at black-and-white television sets propped on boxes. Australian tourists walked in and out, buying cans of Pringles, coconut cookies from China, Snickers bars kept in small refrigerators that cooled nothing. The Vietnamese payed them no mind and adjusted the bent clothes hangers they used for TV antennas. Walt lit a cigarette. There in the humid mist, smelling the dank river, he thought he was back in Watega, drunk on draft Miller Lite from Jarhead's, staggering from his truck and hiding behind the garage and drinking that last airplane bottle before going inside to see Patty in fat-lady's lingerie.

When he pitched his cigarette in the shallow gutter, Tuyen was driving up the street on her Suzuki motor scooter, the white train of her ao dai *wrapped around her waist. Tommy sat behind her and kissed her neck and she smiled and pushed back against his chest. He ran his fingers along her stomach. She laughed and sat erect, her tiny shoulders jutting up, and steered the scooter up the street. He watched them for a long second and wondered vaguely if her dark eyes altered Tommy's world forever. He thought to call out, but right then, among the Vietnamese staring into snowy TV screens, he hated everything about his nephew. They were holding hands and looking at each other. Walt walked off, thinking of the old hopes he'd had the day he left Vietnam, thirty-three years ago, and half-closing his eyes when he understood those hopes were no more than a 1969 GTO. He never had bought the car.*

The small raindrops were muddy from wetting the dust upon the leaves of the plane trees that lined Le Loi Street. A beggar squatted before the hotel, just looking, staring off with a hard face. He had deformed legs, no longer than a dog's hind ones, and walked on his hands between the curb and the hotel gate. His eyes were blue, his face not entirely Asian. Some cyclo drivers were throwing pieces of rolled paper ten steps away from him, then laughing while he ran on his calloused hands for them, thinking them cigarettes. They lounged in the cyclo chairs and laughed big laughs. Walt waited for one to throw another piece of paper before he crossed the street, hoping they'd be laughing at the beggar and not notice him and take off behind him, offering rides to the old city and gibbering about boat tours along the Perfume River.

The weather turned bad after dawn. Walt stood listening to the wind in the trees, sanding the table he'd made from pine boards, soft, knotty wood for practicing. He needed more time before he tried oak. He wasn't fluid enough with the saw and forced his cuts, pushing the boards into the spinning blades, even though he knew he should wait, let the saw take over. The table edges were burned dark. He'd cursed the dog while smoke rose from the saw and the board, then threw the board against the wall and started over. Smooth, he told himself, let the saw do the work.

Ice slanted into the window, but not for long, and by noon, the squalls of rain drove sideways and whelmed the meth smell from the hilltop and turned the trees water black and stripped the leaves off the branches. He knew that the birds had already quit the country at different times, leaving from different places—the pine forest, the hardwoods that walled the river to the east, even the ruined fields—though he'd never noticed their absence until after the first autumn storm made the land stark and smell like cold rain. Then the storms moved down-country, following the river, but the skies remained furious, the sun vague and distant behind the tilting cloud cover, and the wind rose randomly, knocking crooked branches from the trees.

Walt was smoking a cigarette in the doorway when Shirley came walking out of the pines. The wind pushed the boy sideways and the rain drove into his face. He tripped over nothing and knelt hard in the mud. Then he got up again. He reeled backward, glaring at Walt through the slants of rain, his eyes red and heavy-lidded. Walt laughed, his mouth open, blowing cold with the smoke. The kid had wanted to move faster than his legs.

Shirley stopped short of the door. His eyes cast about wildly while the rain made his clothes heavy. Walt stepped backward, but the kid didn't come inside. He pointed at the shed.

"They want to use this for cooking," he said. "Can't do it outside no more."

Walt crossed his arms against the cold.

"No," he said.

"You ain't getting no more money."

"Then tell them thank you."

"They won't even pay what they owe you."

"I said to tell them thank you."

"You got that saw."

"The smell will ruin everything I built."

The kid's eyes narrowed before they inflated. He turned around, took two steps, then turned back. He walked off, talking to himself. He used his hands.

Goofy bastard, Walt thought.

By the time he closed the door, the rain was down to spits. He put two more pine logs in the stove. They hissed on the orange coals while he turned on the saw. He ran a board slowly, very slowly. The sawdust erupted in a fast arc and a fleck spun into his left eye about the time he remembered to put on his safety glasses.

11

Tom Jane came up between two houses in the morning dark, left his rucksack by an oak tree, and crouched low. Jimmy's pickup was parked in the driveway and he saw the cap was open from his loading it for the trip. Tom wanted to take Jimmy from behind, but he was nowhere close. He moved in the shadows the eaves made on the grass. Then an arm went around his throat and his legs were kicked out from beneath him.

"Son of a bitch," Tom said.

"Say *semper fi,*" Jimmy said.

"Is that a town in Florida," Tom said.

"Say *semper fidelis.*"

"I don't speak Italian."

Jimmy started twisting his face as if to break his neck.

"Go on, doggie, say *semper fidelis.*"

"I'd rather have a sister in the whorehouse," Tom said.

"Say it."

Jimmy let go of Tom and they both fell together on the grass and wrestled awhile until they both started laughing. They lay on their backs, breathing hard and watching the last stars fade away over the river trees. They smelled the cold mud from the banks where they'd once fished for bass and bullheads and dreamed outloud of the life before them. Tom sat up first and lit a cigarette and waved it under his nose to kill the smell. Jimmy stood, still catching his breath, and leaned against the house.

"What the hell you doing, Jane?" he said.

Tom sat quietly, studying his hand. The cigarette burned between his fingers.

"That river mud takes me back," he said. "I remember fishing with you down around the trestle. You were going to sail a boat around Africa so you could see the lions come up on the beach. Just the way you read in that book."

"You did a lot of what you said."

"I'm not doing it now."

"I'm the one praying some banker will loan me the money to buy my old man's bar."

"I never wanted to be anything more than a soldier. Now, my dad will get me in that furniture store yet. I'll be pear-shaped by next Christmas."

Jimmy pursed his lips and studied Tom. "Talk about rather having a sister in the whorehouse," he said.

"I don't think Missy would set still for anything less than being the madam."

"Come on, Jane. All I got to do is load my pieces and we'll be ready to go."

Tom stood and brushed the dew off his jeans. He looked at him.

"You said if I came, I could do some hunting," Jimmy said. "What you bringing?"

"My Winchester automatic shotgun. And an AR-fifteen. I

always got my forty-four under the seat. I'm throwing in a Remington eight-seventy pump for you."

"I understand everything but the AR-fifteen."

"For the long shots."

"Shit."

"You got something hid away?"

"Just an H&K forty-five. You know I'd rather watch Little League baseball than hunt deer."

"All that Kraut plastic. You need a Colt model nineteen eleven. A good piece of steel."

"It's the difference between a Mercedes and a Camaro."

"I bet you got excited when we were wrestling."

Jimmy went inside the house and came out through the garage with the two shotguns and the rifle in soft gun cases. Jack, the dog, ran ahead of him toward the pickup and scratched on the passenger door. Goddammit, Jack, Jimmy said. The dog stopped scratching and lay down with his snout flat along the wet gravel. Jimmy lifted up the bench seat and rested the weapons lengthwise. Tom put on his hat and pulled the garage door closed, at which point Jack leapt up and barked until his yellow eyes shook. He reared on his haunches and showed yellow teeth.

"Would you leave the garage door open?" Jimmy said.

"We're leaving town," Tom said.

"I know. But it bothers the dog."

Tom looked at Jimmy and then at the dog.

"He'll be dipshit the whole time we're gone," Jimmy said.

"He's coming with us?"

"You think he feeds himself?"

Tom walked back across the rutted gravel and opened the garage door. Jack went silent and panted, his tongue hanging slack.

Jimmy drove down the curbless street past clapboard bungalows and thin river trees. He stopped after two blocks by the rowed mailboxes for the lane, then looked at Tom like he should know why. Jack lay curled between them on the floor, his eyes closed but his ears perked. Tom drank the bottom from a thermos cup of coffee and looked at Jimmy.

"You waiting on a check?"

"Go back and close the garage door."

"Why did you drive this far?"

"You got to give Jack time to forget about it," Jimmy said.

"You probably give him the steak and eat the Alpo."

They drove west out of Watega County along the state road. The dawn thronged warm light between the layered clouds and the country smoked from the sun upon the dew. The river woods gave way to cut fields and the corn chaff blew across the road and the hedge trees twisted and hissed in the wind. When the clouds broke, the sunlight burnished in the ditch water and bore beneath the visors into their eyes. Jimmy stopped four times to let the dog out, but Jack only sniffed the weeds and barked at the cattails in the bar ditches and then climbed back inside, wet from the tall grass. Jimmy fed Jack beef jerky and scratched behind his ears, and the dog never stopped panting.

"Why can't we take the interstate?" Jimmy said. "We'd be in Hall County before dark."

"You in a hurry to get back to something?"

Jimmy waved Tom away with his hand. "I bet you wish we were doing this on horseback?" he said.

"And we were fighting Indians."

"You'd be the quiet one chewing tobacco and spitting it on Jack's head."

"I'd be wanting to kill the Indians while you were trying to sell them hats and whiskey."

"Selling's more American than killing."

"You sure about that?"

"Shit sure."

Tom refilled his coffee cup from the thermos and lit a cigarette and blew the match out with the smoke. He turned and looked at Jimmy, but Jimmy was watching the wire that sagged between the telephone poles.

"Why you even care about going after Walt?" Jimmy said.

"I don't know. The old man has a bad feeling about him."

Jimmy laughed while smoke puffed from his nose. "That's no news," he said. "Your grandpa's been treating him like a murderer who went free for twenty years."

"It's different."

"Shit."

"The old man sees bad things when he closes his eyes," Tom said.

"Sure. What hell looks like."

Tom rolled down the window and slung his grounds into the wind. "He ever talk about Teddy?"

"No," Jimmy said. "Just every deer season, you wouldn't see much of him."

"Uncle Walt never told me about it. Not even on the trip. But the whole thing was always there, like the trees."

"Men looked at him different," Jimmy said. "I saw it at the bar. Half pity, half fear. Something like that."

"You think that's what sent him off?"

"I don't know."

"Shit, Ruell. You served him beer for eight years."

"He got funny about a year after he caught Sherry with Jeff Brosseau in the garage. Your uncle broke his shoulder with a pipe wrench. Ricky Dugan kept him from being locked up. Brosseau can't even lift his arm over his head."

"Pretty expensive blow job."

"Right before you came home," Jimmy said, "he got the idea to contact his buddies from Vietnam and have a reunion. He brought in these black-and-white photos and showed me all the guys. You couldn't shut him up about it."

"Uncle Walt always told me he left Vietnam in Vietnam."

"He'd drink about three beers and two shots. Then he'd go to the pay phone and take out his credit card and start calling these guys."

"I can see your old man doing that, but not Walt," Tom said.

"He called three numbers every day for a week. A few guys only half-remembered him. He'd stand there at the pay phone describing himself."

It was noon when they drove through Chillicothe County and crossed the Illinois River, which was low from the rainless summer. The driftwood was beached on the sandy banks and the sun streaked faintly upon the brown current. In the sky, ducks flew south in a tight wedge, and along the roadside were the trucks of bird hunters. Often they could see their sandwich bags blown into the hoary grass and hear their distant shotgun reports. This spooked Jack, who twitched and whined and once tried climbing into Jimmy's lap while he steered and smoked. Tom laughed at Jack and took off his hat and put it on his knee.

"I take it he isn't much of a pointer," he said.

"He'll find the birds," Jimmy said.

"He seems too dipshit for it."

"That comes after you pull the trigger."

Tom leaned back and blew smoke from both sides of his mouth. Jimmy pushed the dog back on the floorboards and then looked up.

"Why you prolonging this, Jane?" he said. "We could've been in Hall County by now."

Tom said nothing. He sat with his hands beneath his thighs to warm them. Outside, the yellow sunlight left cloud shadows on the road.

"You can say you don't like being alone," Jimmy said.

"That's not it."

"My ass. When I came home from the marines, it was hard to take a shower without talking to somebody."

"I really rode that kid down at Fort Benning. He was just a weak, fat boy with no business signing up for the infantry. I should have known it and put him in for a training discharge."

"That's on him."

"No. He joined up looking for a father. The same as me. I hated him for that."

"I know a lot of guys who joined so their old man would shut his mouth."

"Does that ever happen?"

"No," Jimmy said.

They drove through the town of Wyanet, where rocky hills rose from the fields beyond the few streets of white clapboard houses and the grain elevator at the railroad crossing. There were bare trees along the hilltops. The afternoon light was orange and even burned pink between the tree trunks, and the few clouds were like handfuls of mud. They found a small crossroads diner near a motel that had been turned into cheap apartments. Six booths inside a plain room, with neither pie in the case nor old men at the coffee counter. They ate skirt steaks and fries with sides of corn and lima beans and looked out at the parking spaces, empty except for Jimmy's pickup and a station wagon assembled from junkyard parts. Tom paid a young woman with fleshy hips that slid in her jeans when she walked back into the kitchen, then teased Jimmy about treating the future Mrs. Ruell so coldly.

The cold wind had come down from the north when Jimmy pulled into a two-pump gas station outside of town. A Buick without a back bumper was parked close to the road. A price of five hundred dollars was soaped into the spider-cracked windshield. There were no gas prices posted, only a sign saying you had to pay first. Inside, a woman in a sweatsuit was scratching lottery tickets and pushing her glasses back up on her nose. Tom paid her and she half-looked at him and said neither thank you nor good-bye. He went outside and pumped the gas and eyed the hills that rose behind the town. Jimmy let the dog run in a stretch of grass between the station and the cut fields, where cornstalks were wound with black dirt.

Tom saw a kid leaning against the station wall by the air hose. He wore a baseball hat and a worn Carhartt jacket too big for him and jeans dirty from sitting on the concrete. He glanced at Tom three times before he walked over with his hands deep in his pockets, then stood by the pump and spat. The wind sprayed the saliva along his dusty sleeve. He looked aloft toward the pole lamps, where the dust moved in fast coils across the white lights. Jimmy was walking back across the lot and cursing Jack for trying to drink old rainwater from a pothole. He reached down and grabbed the dog by the collar and pulled twice before he came. The kid started laughing when Jimmy got to the pickup's door.

"I bet that dog eats his own shit," the kid said.

Tom and Jimmy looked at him and his hard eyes. He was short but looked strong from hard work in the cold.

"I've seen dogs do it," the kid said. "Take a big dump and start eating right then. You got a dog like that, you might as well shoot the son of a bitch, because it ain't no good."

"My dog doesn't eat shit," Jimmy said.

The kid pointed at Tom while he put the pump spout back in the cradle. His fingernails were half-moons of dirt. Pimples lined his top lip.

"Me and him watched your dog drinking that puddle water," he said.

The kid spoke in a high, thin voice that whined and drawled.

"Where'd you learn to talk hillbilly?" Jimmy said. "Nobody sounds like that up here."

The kid looked at Tom like Jimmy was crazy.

"I don't know," he said. "At the learning place."

Jimmy opened the door and the dog jumped inside, his dark dog eyes watching the kid's hands while he fidgeted in his pockets. He was lost in that coat. Tom laughed to himself and stood in the open door.

"Where you headed?" the kid said.

"Up the road," Tom said.

"No shit."

"There you go."

"I was wanting to know if you were going to Hall County?"

"You from there?" Tom said.

"I been to Hall County a hundred times. My cousin's got me a job all lined up."

"Watching dogs shit?" Jimmy said.

"You'd have to be dumb to pay somebody for that," the kid said.

"You know anything about Walter Michalski?" Tom said. "They say he lives in Hall County."

"You give me twenty bucks and a ride and I'll tell you."

"How do I know you've ever heard of Walter Michalski?"

"I could guide you to Hall County," the kid said. "That's worth twenty bucks."

"We got a map."

"I been there a hundred times."

Jimmy and Tom looked at each other over the truck roof. The kid had dirty lips and bad teeth. He nodded at them like what he said made perfect sense.

"You're a damned runaway," Jimmy said.

"You don't know nothing about me," the kid said.

"I don't give a shit about knowing you," Jimmy said. "But you ran off from somewhere."

Tom climbed in the truck next to the dog and Jimmy headed west along the road. The kid stood there in the windy dusk, just the silhouette of him, the dust blowing around him in coils. He did not look after the truck. Jimmy hit the accelerator and headed into the last of the sun.

"Telling a grown man his dog eats shit," he said.

"We could have given him a ride. The kid looked like he'd been eating nothing but candy bars."

"And feed him dinner and put him up in a motel, too. Maybe even find a massage parlor for truckers and pop for a rub and tug."

"He might of helped us."

"Sure, Jane. Helped us get put away for whatever he's running from."

It rained after sunset and cleared within fifteen minutes and the night was almost warmer than the day. The rain was only a mist and never darkened the cement walk outside the motel room. They sat on dusty lawn chairs and the air smelled of field dust, the way it had through the light rain. Jack lay between them on the cement walk with perked ears. They drank beer from a six-pack of long-neck bottles and flipped their cigarettes out into the parking lot and watched the wind take them and blow the sparks like the wake from tracer rounds.

Jimmy crossed his legs at the ankles and then propped one boot heel atop the toe of the other.

"We'd be having breakfast with Walt if we took the interstate," he said.

Tom sat with the beer on his thigh and the bottle was not cold anymore. He was watching the stars above the fields.

"You listening?" Jimmy said.

"I bet a certain housewife in Kentucky wishes we'd been there and back. She's probably got her computer on right now."

Jimmy leaned and spat.

"I shouldn't have told you about that," he said.

"What did you do? Type with one hand and wank with the other?"

"It wasn't like that."

"Nothing ever is."

"Go to hell."

Tom watched Jack twist himself against Jimmy's ankles.

"Was she really three hundred pounds?" he said.

"That's being nice."

"You had no idea?"

"I drove down to Paducah and met her at this truck stop. She was the only one in the place."

"What did you do?" Tom said.

"I turned around and drove home that night."

"She know it was you?"

Jimmy drank from his beer. He nodded.

"You got a new girlfriend?" Tom said.

"I don't want to talk about this anymore."

Tom drew on his cigarette. He held it between his thumb and forefinger and tapped the ash with a quick motion of his middle finger. Jimmy reached down automatically, and the dog licked his hand.

"What we really going to do when we get there?"

"Find a motel like this one and start asking around. Somebody will know him."

"And if they don't?"

"What's wrong with you?"

Jimmy waved him away. The motel light shone vaguely on where the dog had licked his hand.

"Let me have it," Tom said.

"If you could've got back to a Ranger battalion," Jimmy said, "you wouldn't have thought about Walt a second time. Shit, you wouldn't have thought about me twice. You didn't come home for six years. Now all you got left is sitting here trying to convince me to stop wasting my life."

Tom looked at him and his coat, which was dusty from the lawn chair. "That isn't true," he said.

"Walt and I both hate our old man, but we're too scared to shit without asking him where."

"No."

"You weren't raised by a war hero who made a few bucks in a small town. Your old man's hid in his father's furniture store his whole life. You don't know what it's like to have everybody love him and you know what an asshole he truly is."

"My old man and his wife sit around making gingerbread

houses at Christmastime. My mom screws insurance salesmen with Cadillacs, guys who wear gold chains around their necks. Try growing up knowing that."

"At least he didn't expect you to be a killer before you tasted life."

"No. He just expected me to be as pussy-whipped dead as he is."

They sat there quietly and finished their beers and then went inside the damp room. Tom stared at the TV for an hour while Jimmy and the dog lay on the other bed and pretended to sleep.

12

The hotel window was dusty on the outside, and when Dwight looked through it, he did not know where Lake Michigan stopped and the sky started. Down below was an alley where garbage trucks tilted back Dumpsters, and beyond it was Lake Shore Drive, with cars moving like slot racers. The white sunlight glinted off their windshields and the wavelets of the lake and cast shadows of the people who trod them into the sidewalks. He sucked a breath mint and waited for the call girl's knock. She was ten minutes away, but he'd gotten ready early, shaving for the second time that day. He left the money by the room service menu, where the girl would see it.

He'd told the woman at the agency he wanted real tits this time. D cups, big soft ones. He'd driven all the way to Chicago for this, he said, and he wanted things right. The last two girls had had fake breasts, bricks wound in flesh, but once they'd taken off their red bras and matching thongs, he'd gone with things. The woman sent him half of what he wanted. If he complained, the call girl would leave, and he'd be alone with Pay-Per-View pornos. She knew this. No silicone implants, he told her. She even repeated what he said, her voice galled from cigarettes.

When the knock came, he waited a few seconds, then walked over and opened the door. Her breasts were fake, like her fingernails and hair color. He knew by the way they poked against her blouse.

Dwight closed the door behind her and she waited for him to get naked. He smiled and dropped his pants and she put the money in her purse, looking out the window at Lake Michigan. He liked late-afternoon calls because he knew he was their first of the day. She got naked and her breasts were hard as logs. The name Michael was tattooed across her back. A ring pierced her navel. He found himself going with things.

"I don't do Greek or Asian or Russian," she said. "All French with a translator. No kissing."

Dwight stood there naked, looking out the window with her.

"What do you want?" she said.

"A translator?" Dwight said.

She pulled a condom out of her purse.

They did what he paid for. She locked her legs around his waist so he couldn't pound her. Her fake breasts were like sandbags against his chest. He went to kiss her, but she turned away, her makeup spotting the white pillowcase. She kept checking to see that his condom was not slipping off.

"You got a great cock," she said. "I can see your balls swinging."

Forty-five minutes were left after they finished. She curled on her side and looked at her implants in the mirror above the desk, stroking his stomach. He wanted her to see the scar where the dog had bitten him, the cur that'd leapt from the toolshed, crazy from eating rat poison. A cop in Hall County went after dogs that made noise and scared the neighbor kids. She stroked the scar twice and didn't notice, and when her fingernails scraped it again, he tensed and sucked through his teeth.

"I'm sorry," she said.

The girl checked her pose in the mirror.

"It's something the Iraqis gave me," he said.

Dwight waited for her to speak. She touched her left breast and made it even with the right.

"I was a Marine Corps scout sniper. In the Gulf."

"I had a boyfriend in the marines. I model sometimes in San Diego."

There was a digital clock on the TV and she glanced between the time and her breasts in the mirror.

"My position got compromised by this kid looking for a goat," he said. "I had to run in the open. They got me right when I was heading for the chopper. The door gunner was letting loose right over my head."

"He used to sneak me and my girlfriend into the barracks on weekends," she said. "The guys hid us away."

"They wanted to give me the Navy Cross, but the mission was secret. I couldn't even get a Purple Heart. I wasn't supposed to be where I was."

"He still calls me all the time," she said. "He's out of the marines. He's got a car-detailing business in Orange County."

"There really isn't much to killing a man," he said. "The hardest part is not being able to tell people it's not that big of a thing."

"He was Greek. Just crazy."

She lay on her side, looking at herself, goose-bumped from the air conditioner beneath the window. He had time left. He grabbed her from behind, around her waist, and put her on her hands and knees. She went limp like a pillow. He squeezed her waist hard and left finger marks and looked down upon Michael's name tattooed in green ink.

The sheriff's office was hot and near airless save for an oscillating fan that was stuck and blowing dust. Jack Brackett's wet underarms dripped on the brown tiles while he unbuckled the belt around his fifty-inch waist. His jeans were stained with flesh-toned putty from his body shop on Hudson Street, where at night a pellet-gun sniper stalked cats and shot them dead with head shots and broke picture windows and nicked headlights. Dwight waited with the Polaroid camera. Jack Brackett looked around sweat-faced, breathing through his red nose, then scowled. He unzipped his pants and dropped them, his white boxer shorts soaked sheer.

"I can hardly set down," Jack said. "Fucker's the size of a baseball."

"Where's the bruise?" Dwight said.

"It's on my face."

"Let me get a picture."

"This the only way?"

"We need evidence if we catch him."

"I'd shove the pellet gun up his ass and break it off," Jack said.

Dwight swallowed laughter when Jack dropped his shorts. His backside was a snarl of gray hair and pockmarks and the welt from the pellet gun was fist-sized, black as crows. His enormous blue jeans lay around his ankles like an oil spill.

"He sure got you," Dwight said.

"I heard the little fucker laughing."

Before Dwight took the picture, he looked out the window and saw Jerry Bowman parking the big Ford pickup he'd bought yesterday down in Peoria. He honked the horn. The truck was white, with a long cap and two gas tanks, and it had a backseat. The county had repaved the street that morning, and Bowman got out and walked around the truck, looking for tar splatters through his mirrored sunglasses. He really thought he had something. Jack Brackett bent over and half-coughed, trying to pull his shorts up his white legs, when Bowman walked inside, spitting tobacco juice into a Coke can. He leaned against the counter and smiled.

"You got Peek here taking boudoir pictures for your wife?" Bowman said.

Jack got his boxer shorts up with his jeans. He breathed wildly.

"Up your ass," he said.

Bowman spat.

"You'd think a true gift would be her not having to look at it."

"You ever once shut your mouth?"

"Peek would feel unloved," Bowman said.

Dwight sat down behind the desk and put a form in the typewriter. He looked at the Polaroid of Brackett's bruised ass and then at Bowman. He was counting in his head the money the kid had left, fifteen thousand dollars in tens and twenties, buried in army-surplus ammo cans throughout the pine forest, and more came every Tuesday night. All Dwight did was leave a note telling the kid which fertilizer tank was half-full and write a number for the night he'd be on duty.

"Ain't that right, Peek?" Bowman said.

"What did you say?" Dwight said.

Bowman looked at Brackett and rolled his eyes. Brackett stood with his hand on the doorknob and sucked through his nose and mouth. He rubbed his backside.

"It's PTSD from shooting them pigs," Bowman said.

"Shit," Brackett said.

Bowman pointed at his jeans.

"You better get over to Omar the tent maker and think about some new clothes," Bowman said to him.

"Go to hell."

Brackett opened the door and walked out. Dwight listened to him wheezing down the hallway while Bowman laughed, went through the swinging gate, and walked behind the counter. He sat on a desk and looked out the window at his white pickup. He spun the key ring on his finger.

"That truck's better than a blow job, Peek," he said.

Dwight didn't look up from the typewriter. He'd have eighteen grand after tonight, next month double that.

"New?" he said.

"Only a dumb-ass buys a new truck. You let him take the depreciation. Shit, it's damned near new. Only thirty-seven thousand miles. All highway miles."

"Nice truck," Dwight said.

"Next year, I'll be retired and pulling my camper through Wyoming and living on pension checks. Thirty-four grand a year for doing nothing. You'll never have the pension I got. You come on the job way too late."

The lightning wire flared and lapsed when Shirley came hobbling from the roadside, a shadow that swept up against the pale bending weeds rimming the creekbed. Dwight lay in the night heat, his sweat falling against the rifle stock. He was putting the red laser on pine trunks and deadfall and stones with dry green moss. He dreamed himself a fish living in the deepest ocean, long teeth and bulbous eyes. The wind sounded like rain in the weeds. A night bird wagging a pine branch went still.

Shirley came up the creekbed, stooped in a loping run, white from the moonlight leaking through torn clouds. His breath was troubled, his eyes squinting, his ears raised to sort the sounds filling the darkness. The night birds flew. The wind laid down the weeds, then stopped. The quick silence made him scurry; his footfalls were twisted. He came to the rock and put the freezer bag beneath it with the dead grubs.

Dwight let him stand and then the red dot appeared in his left eye. He touched the eye and looked at his hand. He pulled his T-shirt up around his neck. *A skinned spider monkey. That's what the hell he is.* Dwight lifted the dot and fired at a barkless oak. The dead branch broke off and fell on the creek rocks while Shirley clutched his head and dropped to the ground. The red dot made figure eights on his forehead.

"You better kneel," Dwight said.

Shirley was quiet and cut his eyes toward the dead tree.

"You shorted me," Dwight said.

"I was going to make up the money this time."

"Say you know I'll do it."

Dwight spat. He waited.

"Go on."

"I know it."

"Say you know it like your name."

"I fucking know you will."

Dwight moved the red dot between Shirley's wet eyes. They welled in the moonlight. The kid held out his hands toward the trees with splayed fingers as if to ward off evil.

"I'll shoot them off."

"I had to pay somebody to use his land for cooking."

"You dumb shit."

Shirley cried and squinted and teetered on the uneven rocks.

"He bought Leclair's old hunting cabin. Nobody'll smell shit out there. The smell gets you busted."

"I'm the police."

The kid sobbed quietly.

"Say I'm a killer," Dwight said.

He shook the dot on the kid's face.

13

The rain turned warm and quit before the hard winds swept the hilltop. Walt grabbed his binoculars, then stroked down the dog's hackles where he cowered behind the shop door, flecked with sawdust, barking and looking sideways with wet eyes. Funnel clouds were in tumult to the west, attended by a long darkness and a whirlwind scouring the trees below the ridgeline and uprooting hardwoods. Wind-driven sticks reeled up-country with grass shoots and dead leaves. The pine trees bent backward and whipped straight three times. In the fields, where the mud rose from the furrow lines, a corncrib exploded and the gray boards went spinning into the hedge trees along the tractor road.

The skies calmed behind the tornado, but they did not clear. The clouds froze in gray layers like creek ice. He walked out into the rain, and the dog barked from the door when he started down the ridge. Shep held his head straight up and howled. Walt called for him, but he would not come.

He sat on a fallen oak when he got down the hill. The trunk was wide and the broken roots seeped, and the hole it'd left was filled with brown water. Branches littered the creek, and beyond a craggy draw was a line of hickories held only by the grip of their roots. The rain misted his beard and he wondered about the man Teddy would have become. For years, he'd imagined him sweeping the floors in a linoleum factory, taunted by men in flannel shirts and safety glasses. Teddy would keep to his wide broom while they showed him *Playboy* centerfolds, wondering if he got hard-ons. He'd live in state housing and have a social worker who took him to the grocery store on Saturday. They might have Christmas parties for other people like him, hidden away in the basement of Saint Joe's, a few old ladies serving ginger ale and Hi-C punch in plastic cups, maybe a basketball team that played exhibition games against the high school. Some nights, after leaving Jarhead's and taking the long way home along the river, Walt had dreamed he'd sneaked him out of state housing and gotten him a hooker on Washington Street. But the hilltop made things different and they could sit on the fallen oak and watch the wind sucking in the water black trees while they laughed about what a storm can do to woods.

The rain slanted into the hole left by the fallen oak. Walt's face looked back at him from the brown water, where sparrows floated beside an unraveled nest. Their tiny wings were closed and they sank slowly inside the rings made from the drops tapping the brown water. The force of the rain made small wavelets that blurred his face. His eyes wagged. His beard was invisible. He put his hand out as if to push the birds away. The nest turned and bobbed and the birds all went under. He drew back his hand and touched the corner of his eye, then looked off through the crooked branches.

He heard boots sucking in the mud after the wet gunnysack was over his face. A lasso closed around his neck. He went backward and kicked and fought to get his hand between the rope and his throat. He landed on a rock and boots pinned his arms. The click of the pistol's locking hammer and the cylinder turning into place was sharp and clear in the rain. The barrel poked into his eye.

Two sets of hands rolled him to his stomach. His face sank in a mud hole and he sucked groundwater through the burlap. The pistol barrel staved into his skull while he was cuffed. He snorted and the water lifted into his head. They pulled the rope and he came to his knees. His neck veins swelled. He retched water and listened for their breathing but heard only the wind push the rain sideways into tree trunks and tap the dead leaves.

"I'll go away," he said.

Gunmetal slammed his face. He floated and spun circles and thought himself gone from all of it.

They pulled him up the slope, and he slewed in dead leaves to his knees, the limber branches whipping his throat. The dog howled on the hilltop. He tripped over rotten stumps and the rope caught him and he swung around and came to a stop. He hit a small tree and a shower of twigs and rain fell over his clothes. The men breathed hard and coughed, and he tried counting their footfalls. The barking moved closer, the puddles exploding around Shep's forelegs. The pistol fired and all went silent.

"You shot it right out of your hand," a kid said.

They stopped moving and the cold water seeped into his boots. Shep was collapsed in the mud. Walt smelled the burned powder and saw it that way.

"You can't even hold that thing right. You got little bitch hands."

"Fuck you. The handle's wet."

"Shut up." The man's voice was high-pitched.

"Looks like you shit on my gun."

"I told you to shut up," the man said.

They yanked Walt up the broken steps of the shack, his boots heavy with mud. The rain came through the window and tapped the rotten floorboards. They pushed him down and then dragged him by the arm away from the window. Both legs stuck out awkwardly. The cuffs numbed his hands. They cut his bootlaces and taped his ankles together until the roll was gone.

The kick landed under his chin. He bit his tongue while his head banged against the wall. The rope went taut when they tied it off across the room and walked out into the rain. *Shep's hair is wet and straight, streaked with mud; maybe his legs are stretched out to run.*

He sat against the wall until the window square no longer glowed through the gunnysack. The winds came after dark and the tree branches beat the clapboards and the windows frames rattled in their sills. He was mud-soaked and he breathed burlap fibers and coughed in wet gasps. He tried spitting, but the phlegm slid back on his lips. The shack smelled of mold and rotten pine and damp pigeon mote, and when he pissed himself, he welcomed the warmth against his thighs. He leaned forward and raised his cuffed wrists and moved his numb fingers. The metal was lodged into his wrist welts, but that pain had gone before the light went away.

The door opened and light footsteps came across the floorboards. He readied himself, closing his eyes even though he could not see. *There will be no more ideas of myself.* The flashlight shone into his face, the rope loosened around his neck, and the bag came off his head. He saw spots as he blinked and twisted. He leaned back and breathed up the damp and waited for the pistol barrel to touch his skull.

"He should have never brought them kids around. I know them."

It was Shirley. Walt dry-heaved.

"I can't see a damn thing," he said.

The kid turned off the light and Walt sat there, waiting for his eyes to grade to the darkness. Then he saw him. Tall and gaunt, wet like leaves.

"I didn't shoot the dog," Shirley said.

"You were there?"

"I told you: I didn't shoot the dog."

Walt saw part of Shirley's face. His cheeks bore welts. One eye was swollen shut. He held a bag, and the brown paper was rain-streaked and falling apart.

"The motherfuckers beat me with a stick."

Walt looked at him.

"It was my idea, and they beat me."

"Who?"

"Those fuckers he brought around."

Shirley set the bag down. The rain from the open window turned the pigeon dung into white mud and the mote lay in piles like snow.

"You piss yourself?" he said.

Walt was quiet.

"They was going to forget you in here."

"It isn't hard to figure," Walt said. "I know you and you know them. They're going to do something more about that."

Shirley shook his head and tore open the wet bag. Inside were two tins of mustard sardines, bologna, generic potato chips, orange pop in a plastic bottle. It was all slick from the rain. He looked at Walt. His eyes floated.

"Can you just untie me and leave?" Walt said.

"They're everywhere out there."

"You see them."

"He's got these kids with guns."

"Who is this guy?"

"He just wants to cook up a batch. He'll be gone then. Probably the day after tomorrow."

"You that stupid?"

Shirley said nothing. In the darkness, he looked like a kneeling shadow. He made Walt a sandwich and held it to his mouth while he bit and chewed the cold bologna.

14

It was windy after sunrise, when Tom opened the room door and found the kid from the gas station sitting on a parking block, hugging his knees. His eyes cast about like the hedge leaves blowing across the road. The kid looked at Tom and flipped up the collar of his enormous Carhartt jacket. The dust rimed his lips and his teeth were yellow.

"Morning," the kid said.

Tom leaned against the truck and took a cigarette from his pocket and lit it. The kid sat looking at the cornstalks blowing past them and at the motel sign, where the damp husks stuck with the hedge leaves.

"You been out here all night?" Tom said.

The kid glanced out toward the small hills to the east. He stood up and the sleeves from the coat hung down over his hands. He looked earnestly at Tom and chewed on nothing.

"No," he said. "I've been screwing the lady who runs the motel."

Tom turned away, half-laughing, when Jimmy walked outside with Jack. The dog looked sideways at the kid and barked and went to jump, but Jimmy grabbed his collar at the last minute.

"Son of a bitch," Jimmy said.

The kid took a gold pocket watch from his coat pocket. It hung by a chain and he swung it like a hypnotist.

"I'll let you use my watch if you take me to Hall County," he said.

"Just use it?" Jimmy said.

"You ain't got one on your wrist and the one in your truck don't work."

"How do you know it don't work?"

"I've been trying to tell time by it all night."

"But you already got a watch."

"I forgot to wind it. Why else would I be looking in your truck?"

"To steal it," Jimmy said.

"This piece of shit?"

Jimmy opened the door and put Jack inside the cab and the dog growled and drooled on the driver's window. Jimmy looked at Tom and then he looked at the kid again. "I'd bet the same man who's hunting you is also looking for that watch," he said.

"Then I'd be chased by a ghost," the kid said.

Tom and Jimmy laughed openly. The kid left the watch dangling.

"My grandpa is dead," the kid said.

"Why should we bring you to Hall County?" Jimmy said.

The kid rolled his eyes and looked squarely at them.

"Because you're going there and I need a ride," he said.

When they all drove off, the sky was bluer than Tom had ever known, the blue of eyes, and unblurred by the field dust whirling along the horizon. It was warm in the sunlight and made him feel like spring was upon the country. They went through rolling farmland with creeks that cut through the fields, and the cattails were high in the bar ditches. The kid rode in the open bed and sat on the spare tire. He hugged his knees and stared into the wind, his thin body lost in the enormous jacket, which was stained with crankcase grease and dried mortar. From time to time, Jimmy looked in the rearview mirror and shook his head. The dog rode between them and watched the kid through the back window. In the wind, the kid's long hair stood on end. Jimmy snuffed his cigarette in the ashtray.

"We're going to feed that shitbird?" he said.

"I'll pay," Tom said.

"Damn right, Jane."

"He's just a kid. Probably has some stepfather resenting his breath."

"That's your old story," Jimmy said. "His is a lot more evil. I still think we should've frisked him. I keep having visions of the kid putting two in my head at the next stop sign."

"A tomcat could whip his ass," Tom said.

"I don't know."

"I trained a hundred like him down at Benning. He's just looking for a father. They all were."

"Maybe he'll shoot you second for being so understanding."

"You having a Gulf War flashblack?"

"Piss off, Jane."

They stopped at a gas station and bought doughnuts and sandwiches and filled their thermos with coffee. The kid did not talk and slunk down inside his coat. They drove on until they came to some parkland along the Manteno River and turned onto a dirt road, then went along the willows until they found a picnic table by the bankside oaks. The kid climbed out of the bed and Jimmy held Jack by the collar, the hair stiff on the dog's neck. The cuffs from the kid's coat hung well past his hands and he looked like an amputee. Jimmy passed out the sandwiches, two apiece, and fed Jack beef jerky from his pocket. The kid ate greedily, his arm on the table, protecting his food. He cast his eyes about like he was waiting to get hit.

"You just get out of prison?" Jimmy said to the kid.

The kid looked at him and went on stuffing bologna and white bread into his mouth.

"My stepbrother was in Stateville for selling speeders," he said. "He eats like this so some son of a bitch don't come and take his food."

"When was the last time you ate?"

"I had a candy bar and a pop yesterday morning. Right before I met you."

"A candy bar and a pop?"

"I'm really lying to your ass," the kid said. "I had five Whoppers with fries."

"What's your name?" Jimmy said.

"I'm changing it to Richard Head."

"Richard Head?"

"I want to be named after you."

Tom set his coffee down on the initials carved into the table. He and the kid smiled at each other while Jimmy thought over the name as if it were a math problem. The kid went on eating, his arm still guarding his food. Then Jimmy got the joke. He squinted his eyes and shook his head, then pulled out a cigarette but did not light it right away. The kid chewed with an open mouth.

"What's your names?" he said.

Jimmy stared at him and sneered.

"I'm not telling you anything," he said.

"Tom Jane," said Tom. "This is Jimmy Ruell."

The kid nodded like he'd seen them for the first time.

"I'm Marion Butts," he said.

"What'd you do, Butts," Jimmy said, "kill some old couple and steal that watch?"

Butts stopped chewing. He looked out at the river, where the cloud shadows glided across the brown current. Then he went on chewing again.

"My grandpa died, and I wasn't staying around to be took off," he said.

They waited for him to tell more about that, but he didn't. Tom pitched the cold coffee on the dirt and refilled his cup.

"What you going to do?"

"Join the army," Butts said.

"You're not old enough," Jimmy said.

"I can lie right to them about my age. My grandpa said he did it. He fought the Germans when he was just sixteen."

"That doesn't work any more," Jimmy said. "This man here was in the army. He'll tell you so."

Butts looked at Tom and gave him an appreciative nod.

"They'll beg me after they see me shoot," the kid said.

Jimmy picked the crumbs from a powdered doughnut off the wrapper and ate them.

"They hire men like Tom to shut your mouth permanently," he said. "So what you going to shoot then?"

Butts didn't answer right away. He ate the last of his sandwich and scanned the table for more, but there wasn't any.

"Guns," he said. "Revolvers mostly, three-fifty-sevens and forty-fours. I killed a deer one time with a forty-four Magnum."

Jimmy looked up, then went on eating the doughnut crumbs.

"I bet it was dark and the deer was running through the woods," he said.

"Yessir."

"Bullshit."

Butts put the sandwich wrappers in his pocket. He looked at Jimmy and then at Tom. Then he reached in his jacket and made a face, fumbled around and drew out a chrome-plated .44 Magnum with a six-inch barrel and bone handles. He spun it around cowboy-style with his finger in the trigger guard and then set it down on the table so that the chrome glinted in the sunlight. Jimmy and Tom sat looking at the pistol.

"Go on," Butts said. "Pick it up. It ain't loaded."

"You been holding this all along?" Tom said.

"I ain't no magician."

Jimmy grabbed up the pistol and dropped the cylinder and held it to the sunlight. There were no rounds.

"You little asshole," he said.

"I know you all got guns."

"Why didn't you say something?" Tom said.

"Without bullets, it's not much more than a hammer."

"You shoot the old man or the old lady first?" Jimmy said.

"I didn't shoot nobody."

"You kill that deer with this?" Jimmy said.

"I got him below his ear on his right side. At a dead run."

"I don't believe you."

"Get me some rounds and put this handkerchief in any tree without me knowing and spin me around five times with my eyes closed. I'll hit it."

"My ass," Jimmy said.

Butts shrugged and held out his hand for the revolver. Jimmy slapped the cylinder back in place and drew a bead on the tree-tops instead of passing it back. He closed one eye.

"You're supposed to fire a pistol with both eyes open," the kid said.

"I was a marine."

"That don't mean you know shit."

Tom was laughing while Jimmy rose and walked over to the pickup. He kept the pistol. Jack stood with him and trotted on his heels and Jimmy ordered him in the cab and closed the door. He came back to the table holding one .44 Magnum shell. The dog barked and Jimmy told him to shut up twice. Butts was grinning and his crooked teeth were yellow and black.

"One's all I need," he said.

"It's all you're getting."

Butts looked at Jimmy. Tom took the red handkerchief off the table and walked over to an oak tree twenty-five feet away and tied it off on a branch. Jimmy loaded the round and set the cylinder so the hammer would strike the right chamber. Then he handed the pistol butt-first to the kid. Tom came forward and three of them stood in the bright morning light, listening to the river.

"You good to go, Chesty Puller?" Jimmy said.

"Who the hell's that?"

"A hero like you."

"Shit," Butts said. "Then you must be his son Peter."

"I'll count them."

Butts closed his eyes against the sun and turned circles to Jimmy's cadence and kept the pistol hanging before his crotch. It looked absurdly big in his hand. Jimmy shook his head at Tom and swallowed laughter, and when he said "Five," Butts raised the pistol and fired instantly. They were startled, since both thought he'd need longer to find the handkerchief and take aim. The dog was barking. The handkerchief and the branch spun toward the river, and they watched it splash and dissappear with the brown current. Butts held the pistol ready for a long second. He teetered like he was dizzy, and when he turned back, the pistol hung alongside his leg.

"I'll do it all dammed day," he said.

Jimmy said nothing and walked to the pickup and got inside with the dog. Tom looked at Butts grinning and laughed again at him in that immense coat.

"He don't like being showed," Butts said.

"It's a hard way to be in the world."

The kid looked at him like he didn't understand.

"Let me see that pistol," Tom said.

Butts handed it over and Tom threw it quickly out into the river.

"Why'd you do that?" Butts said. "I thought you was the good one."

"I am."

The skies turned gray and cold when they crossed the Papineau River over an iron-sided bridge rusted the orange of the turned hickory leaves. Butts had pulled his head down into the enormous coat and brought his knees against his bony chest like a turtle. The wind battered him and he swayed when the road swerved past a hog farm, the lots made of paintless boards beyond the willow trees, and they laughed while the headless form cursed the reek of pig manure. It smelled of rotten mud and ammonia and wet garbage left cold in the can. Jimmy lit a cigarette.

"I won't cry if that little asshole gets blown into the ditch," he said.

"He's just a kid," Tom said.

"He's not just no kid."

"We'll be done with him by dark."

"It won't be that easy, Jane. He's kind of like shit on your shoe."

"What'd he really do to you?"

"It's more that dirty look he's got. Scares me to think what he thinks about. You know."

"When I was a drill sergeant—"

Jimmy shook his head and blew smoke from his nose.

"Well, you aren't one anymore."

The western horizon was fused with pink and gray when they crossed into Hall County. A landscape of low sandy fields the color of ditch weeds stretched in front of them, and beyond that the hills rose, overgrown with pine and brown brier thicket. A few clapboard houses with yellow-lit windows sprang up from the barren country. The air smelled of trash fires. There were thickets separating the fields, instead of hedge trees, and Tom could see the char marks on the reedy grass where the farmers burned the thicket back every summer. They crossed the railroad tracks and Butts bounced in the truck bed, looking as if he had no head, arms, or legs, and they soon passed a block warehouse circled by a rusted chain-link fence. The sign said WARREN LUMBER and the letters were faded by the wind and the rain. There were old tarps holding rainwater, odd pieces of rotten plywood were strewn about, and many holes had been cut into the fence. They crossed a creek where the water stood green and motionless and the air was rank from chemicals. Tom and Jimmy held their hands over their mouths and noses and their eyes burned. Butts endured the jarring from the bad road while Jack whined and ceased panting for a long minute. A wet-looking dog with one eye limped out of a fence hole and onto the narrow bridge and turned to growl and defend the ruined lumberyard.

"It looks like he's been drinking out of that creek," Jimmy said.

"You think Jack would want to sniff his butt?"

"I hope Walt lives in the pretty part of town."

Tom looked out the window at the lumberyard. There was a lone station wagon assembled from junkyard parts, a sheet of Visqueen serving for a passenger window.

"I somehow pictured this altogether different," Tom said.

"How the hell you know Walt's here?"

"He bought property. You can find that on the Internet just like a three-hundred-pound sex queen."

"Fuck you," Jimmy said.

They were driving up a hillside five miles away from town when a sheriff's deputy turned out of the woods and followed them. He tailed the truck a quarter of a mile before hitting his lights and siren. Butts appeared quickly out of his Carhartt jacket and looked through the back window at Tom while Jimmy cursed and pulled over along the bar ditch. The kid's face was twisted, like he had shooting pains in his gut, and Tom hoped he wasn't carrying anything else in that coat. Jimmy put Jack on the floor and the dog was quiet and lay there looking up with his tongue aloll.

"Now we find out what this little son of a bitch did," Jimmy said.

Tom watched the cop run the plates. His big red face showed in the gray light. It almost glowed. Butts didn't know what to do with his hands. He kept looking at Tom and then at the roadside bushes and the pines beyond them.

"He's a hitchhiker and we're just hunters," Tom said. "We got gun cards."

"And a teenaged serial killer in a stolen coat."

"He's not much more than a runaway."

"This guy's going to assume we're white slavers," Jimmy said. "We're going to be his entertainment tonight."

Looking in the side-view mirrors, they watched the cop step from the cruiser, unsnap his holster, and walk along a sheer wall of cattails. He was their age, with a lifer haircut and spiteful eyes. The fat body he thought was a powerful build was held in a brown uniform with fake creases stiched into the shirt and pants. He had a long flashlight hanging from his belt and he kept an eye on Butts, his hand ready to draw the automatic flapping against his hip. Butts studied the woods, almost pretending he wasn't sitting on a spare tire in the truck bed.

"If that ain't Ron Unger," Jimmy said.

"I bet he's even got ten years in the National Guard."

"And a hundred guns and credit with the hookers out at the truck stop."

"You do the talking," Tom said.

"Just watch me 'sir' this commando right to death," Jimmy said. "Then whip your ass for being so charitable."

The cop stopped by the tailgate and looked cruelly at Butts. He unhitched the gate and pushed it flat with one hand.

"Unzip that coat and throw it down," he said to him. "Then climb down out of there."

The kid didn't even turn around to see who'd spoken. The cop drew his automatic—a Glock .45, as far as Tom could see—then pointed the squirt gun–looking pistol at Butts.

"Kid, you better get that coat off," he said.

"If I throw it in the road, somebody's going to run over it," Butts said.

"You let me worry about your coat."

There was nothing to Butts out of that Carhartt jacket. He seemed assembled from sticks. He jumped down from the gate with his hands on his head like the cop told him and stumbled sideways and then stood in a dirty T-shirt, staring at his shredded tennis shoes. The cop did not holster his weapon. He held it along his leg.

"Now walk up to the front and put your hands on the hood," he said.

In the twilight, the headlights were just beginning to show, and they lit Butts's T-shirt and face and made vague shadows out of the ditch weeds. He touched the hood and pulled away from the heat. He put his hands back and stood looking at the tree line. He shivered and his teeth rattled.

The cop stood behind Jimmy's door, where he could see them all. He breathed like a man climbing stairs. Tom caught the corner of his face in the mirror, made redder by the sun setting up the road.

"Give me your licenses and registration," he said. "Then put your hands slowly on the dash."

They both said, "Yes, sir." The dog looked at the cop and whined.

Jimmy handed over the licenses. Tom watched the cop hold them like two cards and study them in the fading light. Then he looked up at Butts, who'd jumped the ditch and was running like a squirrel for the tree line, his white arms flailing. Tom swallowed a laugh. He was gone into the pines by the time the deputy looked up and said "Son of a bitch."

The cop went as far as the last weed above the flooded bar ditch and stared into the trees where they rose tall and rowed and choked with low-hanging branches. He looked between the woods and the truck five times. Rain drizzled lightly. He glanced a last time out at the dark pines and shook his head. Butts's coat lay in the roadside gravel, the light rain dotting a sleeve.

"Both of you get out," he said.

They assumed the position in the headlights and the cop frisked them with one hand before he said a word.

"Why'd that kid run?"

"He was just a hitchhiker," Jimmy said. "Said his name was Marion Butts."

"The law calls minors runaways, not hitchhikers."

Jimmy said nothing. Tom watched the reflection of the cop in the dark windshield. You took away his body armor, he was just a flabby guy.

"This could take some time," the cop said.

"So close to suppertime," Tom said.

"I get real hungry, too. I can eat for six, maybe eight. I like dessert and coffee. I tip. You should see me tip. Every waitress in Hall County wants to suck my dick."

The deputy had his gun in one hand. He was waiting. The rain glowed in the headlights and marred the webbed dust on the road.

"Silly-looking fucker, wasn't he?" the cop said. "I'd hate to miss supper trying to figure out what you two were doing to him. You might of met him on the Internet. That's federal. I got no way of knowing."

"I'm going to reach in my pocket," Tom said.

"I'm thinking the supper club in Culver tonight."

Tom dropped two hundred-dollar bills on the gravel. The cop walked up behind him and stepped on the notes. He put their licenses on the hood and dragged the bills back with his foot.

"You guys can go."

The cop was staring at them and smiling when they got into the truck. He was still there when they drove off. After awhile, Jimmy spoke.

"You think he had that planned from the start?" he said.

"He saw a business opportunity."

"That little son of a bitch. Running like that."

"He might of made things worse. You think he's got a job here in Hall?"

"He don't got shit anywhere."

15

Dwight held his pistol and watched the pickup's taillights disappear over the hill. He raised his boot and the wind took the bills and they scuttled through the gray roadside grass. He grabbed for them and half-stumbled, but they lifted with a potato chip bag and landed in the bar ditch and went below the dark water. The kid's dirty coat lay balled in the gravel and flecked with rain. He spat and cursed and spat again, then jumped the ditch. The cruiser lights spun blue against the weeds and maimed his shadow.

The kid broke the cattails in the ditch water. His muddy pants stained the goosegrass that snarled along the slope. The rain reeled in the blue light. His trail connected deer lays, where the tall weeds were matted down, and Dwight followed it uphill toward the wood line and wished the mud stains blood trails and dreamed he chased Viet Cong through bamboo glades, the mud warm and steaming, the ground fog lapping ancient jungle trees and marble pagodas swarmed by vines and flowers so red, they held color in the darkness. He flipped off the safety when he approached the pines. The trees ran into a long thicket, woven with brown brier and limber scrub oaks, and to the north was where the river bent near Sugar Island. The kid would have had to turn south to leave the woods and follow the creek that came down the hillside.

The pines grew along the slope in long dark rows. The kid's tracks marred the brown needles and crossed deer prints. The trees were marked from young bucks scratching the velvet off their antlers, and the rain darkened the trees until the marks became vague. Dwight wiped the cold drops from his eyes and worked his Maglite in the tracks. The kid had been heading for the thicket. The wind spun the rain and it disappeared silently into the heaped deadfall. Dwight ran up the slope, slewed in pine needles past his ankles, sucking in the mud. He kept his finger along the trigger guard.

The thicket glowed rain from the flats on the hilltop. He found himself in scrub oaks and evergreens. The slope sheered and the pine trunks were small. The mud had frozen and dried and now was mud again. He saw where the kid had slipped and slid on his hands. Blackbirds sprang cawing from the tall grass beyond the thicket. Then more. They went blurring above the trees, darker than the night, and their sudden flapping spooked him. He slipped on a wet rock and caught himself on a low branch and swung about on his heels. He went backward and the rain bore into his eyes. A shower of sticks and pinecones fell over the brown needles and the branch broke before he came to a stop. He emptied the pistol's magazine into the sky and the muzzle flashes made glowing spots in the night. He tumbled and slid down the hill, the spots pulsating, swarming across his eyes like insects. He lost the pistol and flailed his arms and grabbed at weeds to slow himself. The birds kept coming, their sound not unlike laughter.

Joe and Andy Westerhoff called his father Man of the Future. They got it from their father, Jack, who worked maintenance with him at the Firestone plant. Every guy called him that, even the Mexicans, and the boys didn't know what it meant. Dwight knew his father looked strange with his long fingers and a forehead like a brick and his waist and shoulders the same size. What made the brothers laugh was their father imitating a Mexican accent when he said Man of the Future. All summer they rode behind Dwight on their new bicycles, mimicking their father playing Mexican, and laughing at themselves until they wiped out on front lawns, slapping the air. They told Dwight how funny their father was. He brought dog shit from their yard to the plant and put it in guys' lunch boxes. He spat tobacco juice in Coke cans and offered sips. He did things with Ben-Gay and Icy Hot. All Dwight saw was a guy who drank beer in the driveway, taunting the boys for throwing like girls when they played catch. He laughed because they did.

That summer, Jack quit the Firestone plant and went into business siding houses with aluminum. He bought a white truck and had his name painted on the doors in red letters. He drove off in the morning and came back late at night. He'd wave at Dwight's father from across the street. Hey, Butch, he'd say, tell them they can shove that broom up their ass. He raised his beer in a toast. His father only looked up, his mouth a straight line, then waved back like a robot. Jack wanted to know when he was going to bid days, get out of the graveyard. They have me down for nights, his father said. By late July, the pickup spent half the week parked in the driveway. Joe and Andy kept telling Dwight what a decent truck their old man had bought. The engine hauls ass. You should see when our dad floors it. He races guys in Trans Ams. Just like in Smokey and the Bandit.

One Saturday, Dwight sat in the car and watched his father walk into the Eagle Supermarket. He'd mowed the lawn and his shirt back was wet, flecked with grass clippings. Two teenage girls stood out front, licking Popsicles, their halter tops like wet dreams. They stared at his father's forehead. They watched him through the window as he walked heavy-legged between the sale placards, his knees never bending, his eyes unblinking. One mimicked the way Frankenstein walked, arms straight out, the Popsicle dripping on her hand. They laughed, and Dwight slunk down in the car seat.

There was a Chinese restaurant next to the supermarket, and Jack Westerhoff's truck was parked in front. The place had a small bar. Dwight knew because he walked there nights through the backyards to get his mother chop suey and an egg roll. The bar was cold enough from the air conditioning to hang meat—that was why Westerhoff liked the House of Yung—and one night Dwight had heard him telling the bartender about how they could hang hog quarters, beef sides, long sausage links. He said it over and over while Dwight waited on his mother's order, Jack drunk enough that his eyes trailed off when he looked at things, the ashes falling from his cigarette. It was only Westerhoff and the old Chinese in the pressed Hawaiian shirt who told you how much things cost. The man wiped the bar and sold Jack more draft beer.

You're Butch Baum's kid, Westerhoff said.

Dwight looked at him. His eyes were not straight.

You know how I know? he said.

His chin hit his chest. He never told Dwight how he knew. The old Chinese guy wrote up the ticket for his mother's food, moving his lips and adding the numbers in his head.

Your old man is built for work, Westerhoff said. Cold don't bother him. Works in a boiler room and he don't never sweat. Son of a bitch needs about two hours' sleep. He's like hybrid corn, unfazed by pesticides. Man of the Future. You got to see this guy, he said to the old Chinese. He once took overtime for thirty days in a row.

The man smiled. He didn't understand anything beyond drink orders.

Now Dwight watched his father walk back to the car with a grocery sack. Nothing on his body moved except his legs. The girls looked at the yellow curb, the hockers of gum. They smiled and glanced sideways at each other, swallowing laughter as if air. When he passed them, they broke, and Westerhoff came smoking from the House of Yung. He walked hard. He carried a six-pack in a brown bag, the paper wet from the cans. His eyes swam while he looked at Dwight's father.

Man of the Future, he said. He imitated the Mexicans. Man of the Future, he said again. Built for work. No stopping the Man of the Future.

His father said nothing and held the groceries. He stared off the way he did. Sometimes, for him, the world wasn't there. Perhaps he wished it was dark, the streets empty, like they were when he drove to work through the fields. Westerhoff grinned and showed teeth. His shirt was untucked.

Hey, Butch, he said, you see some monkeys fucking or something?

His father was silent.

Shit, Westerhoff said, a guy leaves and he's like a dead Indian—ain't no luck in saying his name. I bet you all haven't laughed once since I quit. Remember when Ron Roach got hemorrhoids real bad? That fucker was wearing a jockstrap turned backward with a Kotex to keep the Preparation H from staining his shorts. Remember when me and Bruce Blake broke into his locker and smeared that jock with Icy Hot? Son of a bitch."

Dwight's father searched his pockets for his keys, even though they hung from the ignition, glinting sunlight. Then he didn't know what to do with his hands. Westerhoff's arm sweat soaked the bag of beer.

Why you such a goofy son of a bitch? he said.

His father stared off at the lampposts, the white sky, his eyes nearly closed. The teenage girls heard Westerhoff call him a son of a bitch. They stopped licking Popsicles and walked over to see.

Dwight imagined his father picking Westerhoff up and dropping him on his red face, Westerhoff's neck cracking, the loose gravel staving in his eyes. He once thought his father kept a terrible secret. Maybe he'd killed a man with his bare hands, just grabbed him and squeezed his neck until his head hung limp. But he did nothing. The grass clippings on his back were dry.

Westerhoff took the cigarette from his mouth, the filter wet with drool. He studied it between his thumb and finger.

"So am I pig shit to you, Baum?" he said.

When his father opened the car door, Westerhoff flipped the cigarette butt at his head. It bounced off and landed in a pothole.

You a fucking retard?

Dwight's and Westerhoff's eyes met for a long second. They were like two cockroaches trapped in a small space. The teenage girls stood reflected in the store windows, their mouths open, the Popsicles melted.

Don't he talk, kid? Westerhoff said. Probably don't stop to shit or eat, either.

When his father opened the car door, Westerhoff pushed him with one hand. He grabbed him by the shirt, then turned him around. His face was pinched. He dropped the beer and two cans broke open, spraying the back tire. Dwight's father only stood straight and went to get inside the car.

They make your race without balls, Butch? he said.

His father closed the door and turned the key in the ignition. They drove away. Westerhoff swayed and waved, half the buttons missing from his shirt. He laughed big laughs. Dwight looked at his father. He wanted the sunset, a darkness without stars, no sounds save the whistle of the freight train that brought coal to the steel mill in Hennepin, the white light boring through the night over the cornfields.

16

The heavy boot kicked Walt's face and black seeped across his eyes. He squinted against the spots and looked for the starlight where he imagined the window square, but the dark clouds had hooded the night. He went dragging across the floorboards and his cuffed hands climbed along his spine.

He passed through the doorway and his head banged the broken porch boards. They cut the tape from his ankles and pulled him to his feet, and his knees gave and he collapsed down the steps. He rose and slipped and tasted blood. The rope around his neck was cut and the bag came off. Looking across the mud flats, he saw Shirley huddled by the firelight.

Walt tried standing twice before he did. He turned and looked behind him, but the shotgun rammed into his head and stopped him. He'd glimpsed the kid and his hard cheekbones, but not his eyes. He was thin and rain-soaked and his quaking hands made the barrel shake across Walt's scalp until it moved past his ear.

Shirley squatted by the hickory and let the drops slant into his eyes. He wore no shirt and the hair hung from his skull in thin, wet strands. The big kid appeared from the fire smoke with a pistol, his Carhartt jacket made heavy by the rain, then whipped Shirley across the face. His hands were like field rocks. Shirley sat rigid in the smeared firelight and stared at the hot logs hissing steam, his bare chest mud-lathered from being dragged. The big kid palmed Shirley's skull and shook it until his mouth opened. He fired twice over his head, the rounds shattering a charred log, then wiped the hot barrel across his lips. Shirley let his tongue wag.

Walt was looking down at Shep when the cuffs came off his wrists. The dog lay in a puddle, his legs stretched out like he was running, and the rain straightened his hair. Then the shotgun poked Walt's head, forcing him toward the fire. The moonlight set in a vague swale down the hillside, shifting and darkening when the clouds jelled to the east. The big kid looked over at him. His eyes were almost shut against the rain. His stuffed face was colored like putty.

"You two are going to fight," he said.

His teeth rattled after he spoke and then his mouth snapped shut. He smelled of chemicals.

"No," Shirley said.

"The fuck you ain't."

"He said you can't."

Shirley watched the fire. His face was drained. The big kid grabbed his neck like a kitten and stood him up on his bare feet. Shirley thrashed about, trying to sit down, and the kid thrust him out of the firelight.

"Come on, you little bitch," he said.

Shirley covered his face with splayed fingers.

"I see you playing them video games," the big kid said. "Talking about killing every motherfucker that moves."

The shotgun fired over Walt's head. The hot brass from where the shell had been ejected burned his hairy back. He saw his shadowed paunch reel in the mud. The butt stroked his kidney and he flexed backward. His boot struck Shirley's groin and the skinny kid fell back, fending him away with stick arms. Walt swung with open hands and the blows slid across the Shirley's face. Blood leaked from the corners of his eyes. He tried hiding in the shadows. Walt teetered and then stayed himself. The cold breath rose from his mouth in gouts. Shirley fell on his knees and his backbone raised and the skin sucked between his ribs. He would not fight.

The kid took a handful of Shirley's hair and pulled him up. His eyes bulged and his lips curled over his teeth. The fire died to steaming coals. The kid put the pistol against Shirley's temple and pulled the trigger. Shirley's neck yanked straight from the force of the round. He caved in upon himself. He died with open eyes. The kid laughed, his mouth open. He howled while the rain disappeared into his head. Then two shotgun slugs tore open Shirley's hips and spun his body.

In the darkness, Walt could tell no difference between the blood and the runny mud. He was afraid to exhale. The kid with the shotgun gave a wet cough and ran the barrel along Walt's spine. Walt reeled and thought nothing of finding his balance. The cold was deep inside him. The hazed moon burned in a distant corner of the sky.

The kid was rolling Shirley's head beneath his boot when a short man came running from the pines. He held his side. He was covered with dead leaves, wheezing from the uphill run. The kid pushed the head down into the mud and the blood stopped pulsing. His eyes were shadowed crescents with nothing there at all. He looked over at the man.

"The fucker wouldn't fight," the kid said. "I ain't lying."

The man put his hands on his hips. He bent over and dry-heaved. His soft body bounced beneath his police uniform. An empty holster hung against his leg. He looked up and opened his mouth, but no words came. He stood straight and his breasts poked into his shirt. The kid pointed at Walt with the pistol.

"But this one started slapping the shit out of him right away," he said.

"No," said the man. His mouth was red.

"He was fighting right off," the kid said. He jerked his head toward the one with the shotgun. His teeth appeared and then went away. "Ask him."

The man looked at Walt and the kid looked at him and the rain turned the last fire ember black. When the man knelt to touch Shirley's head, the kid scowled, his face red, and swung the pistol and knocked him sideways. A gout of blood flew from the man's mouth. The kid knelt on his back and grabbed a handful of hair and jerked his head up. He dunked the man's face in the mud and the man spat and sucked air through his nose. His mouth hung open and dripped filthy water. Walt watched the rain fall straight down and saw the water run dark in the gullies and culverts and the rocky draw that went somewhere he didn't know.

The boys beat them toward the shack and grinned with twisted faces and laughed like idiots. The kid with the shotgun took turns butt-stroking their kidneys and tailbones. He was saw-toothed, his eyes bright like china, and he waved the barrel in arcs before their faces. The big one swung a baseball bat at the rain and prodded the man, miming sodomy, and the man made sounds not unlike crying and high-stepped through the puddles. They lurched up the stairs and the boys cuffed them back-to-back and left them with their knees raised against the cold. The rain drummed the roof and came through the windows, and the pigeon dung became a reeking white fluid that pooled upon the floorboards. The birds perched upon the rafters whirred and shook their wings and their mote fell upon both men's faces.

The man cocked his shoulder blades against the chill. He coughed dryly, and Walt felt his insides lift and heave. Three shotgun rounds sounded ahead of laughter like hard kicks. They fell to their sides and lay on their ears while the slugs hit trees and the branches curling over the roof and the one window frame holding glass. The man ground his teeth. Walt listened to the pigeons' wings cutting the cold darkness while they rose through the hole in the roof. *If Teddy'd lived, he'd just be kept hid somewhere, and the old man would never have shut up about that.*

17

Tom Jane sipped his coffee and walked along the bar ditch and went back to the motel room. There was no vacancy sign, only the metalwork that had once held it over the pop machine. He sat on the tailgate of Jimmy's truck and smoked in the morning dark while a freight started over the tracks. The engine lights flashed in the motel windows. The boxcar doors were open, and looking through them, he watched the country pass by. He was still watching it when Jimmy came outside with the dog.

"You are one heavy bastard," Jimmy said.

"Come get your coffee," Tom said. "The motel office sells it."

Jimmy sat down on the gate and took the lid off the coffee, and the steam fumed around his face. Jack lay down by his boots. Tom grinned and put the cigarette he was smoking in his mouth, drew deeply, and then exhaled through his nose.

"I used to sit in my truck outside the barracks a half hour before first call and do this," he said. "I'd drink coffee and watch the last fireguard's flashlight in the windows. Then I'd wake up Joe with a garbage can and a baseball bat and run him until he drooled and forgot the time of day."

Jimmy rolled his eyes and scratched gravel against the pavement with his boot. Tom stubbed out the cigarette and held the butt a long second before putting it in his coat pocket.

"I was something then," he said. "So was Joe. Now I'm just out here."

"Missing another war. They'll spend a billion dollars blowing up some two-dollar tents."

Tom was quiet and drank coffee.

"That was a joke," Jimmy said.

"I know."

"You tried to do good by taking Walt there."

"I don't know. Maybe I brought something on."

"Walt came home and didn't have Vietnam anymore."

"He had a good time."

Jimmy worked Copenhagen against his gum, then spat. Tom lit another cigarette, stared at the ember, and let the ash grow long.

"Remember when my mom was married to that son of a bitch?" Tom said.

Jimmy drank and nodded.

"You ain't going to talk about how Walt saved you on the weekends by taking you out to work?"

"He did."

"Walt had you cutting down trees on that lot he bought by the river and he never gave you five bucks."

"He used to teach me things."

"How to hold yourself in a bar."

Tom Jane said nothing. Jimmy spit snuff off his tongue.

"What do you know about Walt anyway?" Jimmy said. "It isn't like he ever gave much of a shit about you. The guy's first love was booze."

They drove into Hall while the autumn morning came cold and the wind blew from the north, where the wooded hills rose against the cloud cover. There was a town, even if nobody went to it anymore. The block of storefronts was vacant above the curbless street and the VFW post had unlit neon beer signs in the basement windows. Barn pigeons roosted on a power line that sagged above the rooftops and dripped last night's rain. A green pole stood at the street end, where the stop sign had been stolen. Behind the town was a white-board church, and the pigeons flew between the power line and the steeple and shat white upon the bare wickerwork of trees lining the back lots.

Jimmy slowed and Tom studied the diner, where a light paled the wet window. Two Mexicans stood quietly in the doorway, their coveralls stained with field dirt. Tom looked at Jimmy.

"I guess this is as far west as a broke plumber gets," he said.

"Life's out by the interstate these days," Jimmy said. "You find the Wal-Mart and you'll get the rest."

They crossed railroad tracks with neither lights nor gate and left town on a road that was unswerving and empty of traffic. The cut cornstalks lay stitched with the field mud, half-drowned, and the wind blew lines in the standing water. The road veered north and then went east through a glade of oaks with wonky branches made black by the rains. Tom cursed while situating his legs to accommodate the dog, who lay sprawled on the truck floor.

"Why's this dog up my ass?" he said.

Jimmy laughed and hit the wipers against the small mist.

"You're in his seat," he said.

They came to the lumberyard with the fetid creek, but the dog was gone from the weedy banks. Tom nodded for Jimmy to pull into the lot and Jimmy half-winced and turned the wheel. The tires scratched the lot gravel and bounced over the deep ruts. The light lit the glass door, and the tarps covering the two-by-fours held water where the fabric sank between the boards.

"You see anybody in town to start asking about Walt?" Tom said.

"No."

Inside, the old man totaled numbers on an adding machine, its tape curling against the floor. Coarse gray hair twisted from his ears. He held a pencil like a cigarette. The store shelves were scratched and empty and the carpet was red like the man's jacket. It was burned from cigarettes and spotted black with chewing gum. He eyed them from an oaken swivel chair and held the receipt tape between his fingers.

"I can order you anything you want," he said. He continued working and nodded at three catalogs on the counter. They had no covers. "Three days," he said.

"At least you speak English," Jimmy said. "I didn't see anybody in town who'd know what hello means."

The old man looked at him over his glasses. One bow was bent from where he took them off.

"I fought in Leyte so Bill Clinton could turn Hall into a suburb of Nogales, Mexico. I sure the hell did. That's what it was all about."

"I was wondering if you could help us?" Tom said.

The old man smiled thinly and chewed on nothing. "I can't afford to buy Little League uniforms any more," he said.

"No," Tom said. "It's not that. I think my uncle moved up here in the summer. His name's Walt Michalski. He has a beard and real blue eyes and owns this coon-faced dog."

The old man looked at the empty shelves and then at Tom.

"Looks like he ran off a long time before he ever thought to run?" he said.

"Does he drive a green pickup?"

"With a tailgate that falls down every time he hits a pothole," the old man said.

"That's him."

"He bought a useless hilltop about twelve miles from here. Nothing but scrub pine and thickets. I sold him all his concrete and lumber. He said he was building a woodworking shop and hanging out a shingle in the spring. I wished him luck. You can't even sell these Mexicans toilet paper."

"How do I get out there?"

"Just head back west and turn north on One nineteen. Take the first gravel road about six miles and you'll see his dirt road. Come winter, it's hell out there."

Tom wrote all of it down.

"You need me to draw you a map?" the old man said.

"No."

"I draw a good one. You won't even know you're lost."

The road the old man spoke about took them along a creek. The water was the color of asphalt. The current was swift and the water broke white over cast-off tire rims and a refrigerator door. The wood line ran back from the road, and the plain was overgrown with prairie grass and reddish sorghum. Beyond the trees were house trailers grimed by the sandy dirt of the country. A corncrib with gray boards stood in the field, weeds growing to the rotten eaves. They smelled leaf fires and pigeon dung and the stagnant ditch water, where cattails stood like stick men.

"Son of a bitch," Jimmy said.

There was hitchhiker at the curve a quarter of a mile away.

He'd been sitting, but he stood when he saw the truck. The wind drove the light rain into his head.

Tom sat up and looked. "That's Butts," he said.

Jimmy spat into an old pop can.

"Does he see us?" Tom said.

"Now he does."

Butts ran out into the lane and waved both hands like an umpire.

"We can't leave him out here," Tom said.

"The hell we can't," Jimmy said.

He sped past the kid, then looked in the rearview mirror. The wind ran in the cattails and Butts stood there watching. Jimmy slowed the truck to a halt.

"God damn you, Jane," he said.

"We got to at least get him on his way."

"You're winning the grand prize of shit here."

"I know."

Jimmy shook his head and reversed the truck, looking over his shoulder and steering by the yellow line. Butts ran to meet them. He wore a fat woman's coat of brown wool and it rose behind him from the wind. Jimmy looked at Tom and then looked away, rolling his eyes. The dog climbed up on the bench seat to see. Tom opened the door, where Butts stood breathing heavily and pointing back up the road. He looked like a runaway monk.

"I must have ESP," he said. "I was thinking about you two and here you come."

"Where'd you get that coat?" Tom said.

"Same place I got dog-bit."

Jimmy Ruell blew cold and looked off at the wet trees. The rain had quit, but the branches dripped.

"No lie," Butts said. "I got dog-bit."

The kid opened his coat and on his T-shirt were teeth marks and dried blood.

"The son of a bitch knocked me down and bit me," he said. "Missed my heart by nothing."

"What did you do?" Tom said.

"Knocked that dog silly. I don't think he'd ever been hit before, the way he rolled over."

"No," Tom said. "To make him bite you."

"Nothing. He just come over and bit me. I was going through a box of clothes sitting behind the church. I found this hat."

He held up the hat. It was a Day-Glo hunting hat with drop-down ear warmers.

"Why'd you run from that cop?" Jimmy said.

Butts put on the hat. His ears were red from the cold. The hat was too small and he was pulling it down over a thick head, which didn't match the rest of his body.

"It'll only warm the top part of my ears," he said.

"You cost us two hundred bucks," Jimmy said.

"I'm good for it."

"Shit."

Tom was laughing at Butts in the coat. It had no buttons and he held it closed like a woman would a robe.

"You get my Carhartt back?" Butts said.

"No."

The kid frowned in the wind.

"Then borrow me a rope so I can keep this son of a bitch shut."

"I need to know a few things," Jimmy said.

The kid was quiet, but he watched Jimmy. One eye crossed. He hadn't been to sleep.

"I told you," he said. "My grandpa died and I wasn't waiting around to see where they'd take me."

"You got nobody in Hall County."

Butts shook his head. "I just heard of it before," he said. "They got this big fair in the summer. The monster trucks come and everything."

"Where you figuring on going?"

"Not to no home full of mouthy blacks. No family is going to take me after what I've done."

Tom and Jimmy looked at him.

"I've broke stuff."

"You got any ideas what we're supposed to do with you?" Jimmy said.

The kid didn't say anything. Then he said, "Hire me to teach that dog not to eat shit."

They drove off with Butts sitting between them. The dog watched him from the corner of his eye. The kid smelled of dried rain and brackish ditch water and his back was filthy from the forest dirt after spending the night in the hickories beyond the road. He put the hunting cap on his knee. His mouth hung open and Tom didn't think he could close it.

"You don't got nothing to eat, do you?" he said.

Tom opened the glove compartment and gave him two packages of chocolate doughnuts and a Little Debbie brownie. The kid chewed with a smile.

"These here are from Jimmy Ruell's private collection."

Butts nodded and swallowed and the crumbs dropped where the blood from his dog bite had dried. Jimmy said nothing and squeezed the steering wheel. Tom saw that the kid's top lip was fat, and beneath the grime and blackheads riming his cheeks were thin brier scratches.

"What happened to your face?" he said.

"You wouldn't believe it."

"No, we won't," Jimmy said.

The kid cleaned the chocolate off his teeth with a finger and then ate the residue.

"That cop chased me through the woods and tried killing me," he said.

"Before the dog bite?" Jimmy said.

"Hell."

The kid looked at him with flared nostrils. He spoke with a full mouth. "I slipped and fell into a thicket, but he slipped and fell on his ass and started shooting up the sky."

"Then you started teasing the dog," Jimmy said.

"I never teased no dog. It just come up and bit me."

The road was empty and they drove through the hills and then went down a long hillside into a small valley. There were woods on both sides of the road. Looking through the bare trees to the south, Tom saw the Manteno River, the water muddy, slow, and deep. The river was high and wide and there were tiny islands with hardwoods and thickets and a long sandbar that stretched down the middle. He saw old limestone bridge piers where the river bent from view and they passed an old clapboard house beside an apple orchard overgrown with scrub oak.

Butts fell asleep and his head rose and fell with the road. Thin streams of drool leaked from his mouth corners. His face was a mosaic of dirt and acne and patchy whiskers. He smelled as if he'd been wet for a long time and then dried in the cold.

Jimmy cracked the window and shook his head but said nothing.

They found the gravel road after dropping down into another small valley. There were hills to the east beyond the river, but the highest range rose in the west, brown and dark and vaguely green against the pines. Jimmy took the road into the woods and followed fresh tire tracks, and many times low-hanging branches scraped the pickup's roof. He drove slowly and the gravel was too wet for dust to rise. Sunlight broke through the cloud cover and, looking through the tree trunks, they saw light shimmer upon the river. Butts snored and phlegm rattled in his throat.

The first dirt road they passed climbed up a hillside. Rain stood in the tire ruts where a truck had been stuck. Jimmy slowed the truck and looked out the window. A thicket ran on both sides of the road and brown briers dripped old rain.

"We ain't driving up it," Jimmy said.

"Keep going. We can walk up the hill from the back."

"Don't get into a big pissing contest with Walt."

Tom nodded. Jimmy took the gravel road around the hilltop.

"The old man give you a tranquilizer gun to get him home?" Jimmy said.

"No."

"What the hell you going to tell Walt anyway?"

"I'm leaving the talking to you. You're the bartender."

Jimmy drove a half mile and parked in scrub trees that overlooked a cut field. There were pines on the hilltop. They smelled the river even though they did not see it. Butts slept with his head on Tom's shoulder.

"What about my little brother?" he said.

"He's coming. We'll leave Jack. Otherwise, he'll hot-wire the truck and sell my dog to the Chinese."

Jimmy kicked the kid's shoe and he came awake fighting. He swung his fist and Tom caught it like a baseball. His eyes were half-closed.

"It's only you all," he said.

"Who'd you think?" Jimmy said.

"You don't know shit right when you wake up."

"I just think you don't know shit."

They got out of the truck. Butts stood there in the enormous coat.

"Smells like cat piss out here," he said.

"That's you, chief," Jimmy said.

"Damn, it smells. You got a rope?"

Jimmy flipped him a bungee chord out of the toolbox.

"What the hell am I supposed to do with this?" he said.

"Run it around your waist and hook the ends together," Tom said.

"You think your dad will have any more of them dough-nuts?"

"It's my uncle."

Butts looked around and nodded.

"You think he will?"

Jimmy led them up the ridge, like he knew where was going. Tree trunks rotted on the sandy ground. They did not move in a straight line, but went left and right, going the way the trees had fallen. Tom watched Jimmy's lanky figure recede into the dark pines ahead. Blackbirds were coming up the hillside from the fields south of the road. Tom heard them cross overhead but didn't look up. He waited on Butts. The kid came through the brier with his hands before his face like a boxer. He panted. His jeans were filthy from tripping over vines. After awhile, they caught up with Jimmy. Butts spat.

"What's his problem?" he said.

"You got to keep up," Tom said.

"I ain't no deer."

Jimmy looked at them from the pines but didn't speak. The wind shifted and gusted down the treetops. He put a finger over his mouth. He smelled and listened.

"You smell ammonia?" he said.

"I told you it reeked here," Butts said.

Jimmy eyed the kid cruelly.

"It gets real bad when the wind jumps," he said. "Like strong cat piss."

"That's what I told you," Butts said.

"Shut your mouth," Jimmy said.

"I don't smell anything," Tom said.

"Wait," Jimmy said.

Tom heard the wind in the pines before he felt it sting his face. His eyes bleared.

Jimmy walked ahead slowly and then put up his hand. Tom knelt behind a fallen oak while Jimmy crouched in the thicket. The wind ran in the pine trees, and after the rush, Tom heard footsteps breaking sticks.

"What the hell?" Butts said.

Jimmy turned and glared at them for quiet. Tom had forgotten Butts. He grabbed him by the arm and pulled him down so Butts faced the opposite way from the noise.

Two kids stepped out of the trees, one of them carrying a shotgun by the receiver. His face jerked while he peered down the hillside, as if looking into bright light. The other kid was thicker and swung a baseball bat at the low-hanging pine branches. Pimples coiled upon his cheeks and he wore the kid's Carhartt Jacket, which fit him tightly. Butts twisted his head so he could see over his shoulder before turning himself around.

"That son of a bitch is wearing my coat," he said.

Tom Jane grabbed him by his T-shirt or he'd have run at them. "What you going to do?" he whispered.

"Get my coat."

"Set down."

Before Butts moved, Jimmy picked up a rock and glanced at Tom and then pointed down the hillside. He had three more rocks gathered by his knee. Tom kept hold of Butts while Jimmy threw a rock at a pine tree about twenty feet from the kid with the shotgun. The kid shouldered the weapon and his camouflage pants slid down his thin waist. It was an automatic with a black plastic stock and was good for three shots. The thickset one raised the bat and they both moved toward the sound. Jimmy threw another rock and sent it a long way into the forest. The kid drew down on the sound and fired two shots very fast. The red shells ejected into the gray light. Jimmy hurled the final rock and the kid shot the last round. There was shouting from the woods.

Tom pulled Butts to his feet and they went running down the hill. Butts tried breaking away but tripped over the train of his coat. Tom took the deadfall like a hurdler. Three pistol shots came from somewhere in the woods, all evenly spaced. He stretched his legs and let go of Butts. More shots were fired and they hit close enough to fell a hickory limb. Blackbirds jumped, cawing, and all was lost to bird sounds. Jimmy passed them both, his long legs nimble over the deadfall. His baseball cap flew off his head.

When they reached the bottom of the hill, the shotgun was firing from the woods. They ran for the truck along the gravel road. The dog barked and threw himself against the windows.

Pistol rounds gored the tree trunks. They climbed inside and Jimmy drove off in the opposite direction from where they'd come. The pickup fishtailed in the soft dirt and light rain streaked the windshield. The kid fired the shotgun from his hip. He was out in the open. The dog jumped on Butts's lap and howled at the back window.

"This is where that cop tried to kill me," Butts said.

"Shit."

"You know where you're going?"

"Shut him up," Jimmy said to Tom.

The road graded before he could say a word. There were fresh tire ruts. The ammoniac smell was very strong and made their eyes water, and Tom saw the trees as if through wet glass. Beyond the thicket was a shacklike house and a new garage. Cast-off boards and a hundred spent shotgun shells lay in the mud. Jimmy pulled a U-turn and the truck slid and almost went into a draw. He took his .44 Magnum from under the seat and passed it to Tom by the long barrel while the dog pinned Butts and he flailed his arms. Tom Jane said nothing, rolled down the window, and leaned out, holding the heavy pistol with both hands.

The kid was loading the shotgun when they drove back down the hillside. He stood in the road and fumbled with the bolt. He could not lock it back. When he looked up, his face wound tightly over small cheekbones, Jimmy hit the gas and Tom let go one round. The kid dropped the shotgun and jumped into the ditch while a pistol bullet chinked the pickup bed. Tom swung around and fired twice into the woods, and he could hear the shooter's bullets going high over the truck's roof. Jimmy swerved and tried running over the shotgun. Butts panted like the dog and struggled.

Soon they were back on the gravel road and speeding between hilltops. Jimmy steered and kept his head down. A gel of slate clouds gathered to the east and had already darkened the country. The rain rolled down the windshield. Tom kept watch, with the pistol hard before him. Jimmy hit the wipers and turned on to the blacktop.

"That was Walt's shotgun," Jimmy said. "He bought that Benelli off Larry Anderson right before you come home."

"You know for sure?" Tom said.

"That's a thousand-dollar shotgun."

The dog calmed and Butts spat on the floor. "They're cooking meth up there," he said.

Tom brought the pistol back inside the truck and looked at him.

"That's the cat piss smell," Butts said. "Remember how it got real strong when we saw them houses?"

"How do you know?"

"The shitsack's right," Jimmy said. "It's meth. You see that new garage?"

Tom had seen it.

In the motel room, Tom and Jimmy sat smoking on the beds while the wind tore through the country and the rain came down in sheets. Tom rubbed his head, which ached from arguing with Jimmy. Butts slapped the sides of the television, trying to clear the snow and broken lines, and cursed over the hissing sound and kicked the dim-lit air. A long, rolling crack of thunder went down the sky to the west, the nightstand light flickered, the TV popped black, the bulb in the lamp dimmed to a thin orange wire, and then all was dark. Butts turned the power knob off and on five times before Jimmy snuffed his cigarette in the glass ashtray and looked up from the bald carpet.

"Sit your bony ass down," he said.

The kid's stringy hair was wet from the shower and he combed it with his fingers. He'd put his dirty clothes back on and stank like field mud. He walked over to the bed, where the dog lay beside Jimmy, and the dog rose, barking when he tried sitting down.

"Not here with them dirty clothes," Jimmy said.

Butts went back to the TV and started turning knobs. "I like watching dance shows," he said.

"I told you to sit down."

"I ain't sitting on the goddammed floor."

Tom Jane smoked. The pain was right behind his eyes.

"Go easy," he said.

"Go easy shit," Jimmy said.

Butts leaned against the wall and jacked a leg against it. "You two ain't starting again," he said. "You know how long it's been since we ate?"

Tom looked at Jimmy. He was watching the rain slash down the window glass. "What's our choices but going and getting him?"

"Dammit, Jane," he said. "It's a police problem."

"You saw the police."

Butts stood nodding. His muddy pants were dried hard. "The police tried killing me," he said.

"Shit," Jimmy said. He then looked at Tom and held an unlit cigarette. "You probably think they got Walt tied up and laid over train tracks," he said. "Everybody knows Walt dealt coke. He's right in there with them."

"What do you think?" said Tom.

"I think you want to play sergeant to shithead over there."

"I ain't afraid of no tweekers," Butts said.

"I'm out, Jane."

"Then why aren't you gone?" Tom said.

Jimmy Ruell didn't answer. He lit the cigarette. They sat for a long time and nobody said a word. After awhile, Jimmy lay back with his cigarette and Tom watched the ash fall upon his face.

18

At dawn, Dwight lay listening for their boots in the mud after the shooting stopped. He glimpsed the corner of the man's eye from his own. Their scalps and spines touched and their bodies were no longer warm. The rain slanted through the holes in the walls made by the deer slugs and the drops were loud in the puddles. The pigeons came back to roost upon the rotting crossboards beneath the roof. One by one, they descended through the ceiling holes and whirred and twisted their necks strangely and fought with their beaks for roosting space.

He looked up through the window. The stars went mute in the hem of sky above the river trees while the dawn became morning. The birds shat dirty white lumps upon their heads. The man coughed and spat and ground his teeth.

Dwight was silent and lay in the water and listened to it leak through the floorboards. In the grainy light, the rain was half-visible as it fell with the pigeon mote. He sensed that the man was thinking when the shotgun fired three times by the road and then an engine sounded in the rain ahead of spinning tires and the fast shots from a heavy-caliber pistol. The pigeons exploded and collided and fell to the floor and hobbled about with flapping wings. They flew dazed and many hit the dripping crossboards on their way through the roof holes. The man's skull scraped his own while he watched the birds. His body was limp. He strained his neck to see the last pigeon fly away.

The big kid, named Russell, came running inside without a coat. His eyeballs snapped and he waved the pistol and muttered half words. Screaming, he threw himself into the wall. The man was whispering to himself. The kid sat in a puddle and looked at Dwight and howled. His tongue wagged. He beat his heels on the floorboards and pointed the pistol at Dwight and lay back, laughing.

"They beat him until he shit," he said. "A hundred niggers with knives did."

The kid stood and fired without aiming. The round nicked Dwight's shoulder and smacked the floorboards. The pistol clicked when he pulled the trigger again. He looked at Dwight blankly and ran laughing from the shack.

"Niggers everywhere," he said. "Niggers coming in trucks and breaking loose through windows. Running like sons of bitches."

Dwight felt the blood dilute on his wet arm. The man was very still and did not breathe, but Dwight felt his heart beating where they lay back to back while outside the wind bent the rain. He waited for the pigeons.

19

Jimmy Ruell's truck was parked in the woods where a field road came through the poled oaks. The moonlight sleeved the tire ruts and smeared the young trees and shadowed the old rain dripping from the branches. Tom Jane put the .44 Magnum in a nylon shoulder holster. His face was black from shoe polish and he had cut the fingers off his gloves. Butts sat on the tailgate, having just finished with the polish. He wore Tom's army field jacket and the coat swallowed him and the sleeves were rolled above his hands and pinned to stay up. Jimmy squatted inside the wood line with the AR-15 across his knees and stared off. Tom gave Butts spare Magnum rounds attached to speed loaders.

"You need more practice using these things?" he said.

Butts looked up with his mouth open. The kid's legs dangled from the gate, his toes sticking through his tennis shoes.

"When do I get a gun?"

"You need one yet?"

Butts reared back his head. "What if you both get shot and I'm all alone?"

"Then run like hell."

Jimmy smoked and hooded the ember with his hand. He stood with the rifle and leaned it against a tree. "I feel like a fool," he said.

Tom made Butts jump up and down to see if he rattled. He looked him over for anything that shone. The kid checked out.

"You hear me, Sergeant Jane?" Jimmy said.

Tom looked over his shoulder. He was rubbing shoe polish behind Butts's big ears. "Why don't you wait by the truck," he said.

"We're not with the government."

"Then sit here and sing radio songs."

Jimmy opened the truck door and got inside. He turned the key and scanned for an FM station. Butts chewed on nothing and gawked at Tom with his head held sideways.

"He a chicken?" Butts said.

"Shut him up, Jane."

"You'll be here?" Tom said.

"Yeah."

Tom and Jimmy looked at each other for a long second and Jimmy turned away first.

"You know Walt can't help shitting in his mess kit," he said.

"You'll be right here?" Tom said.

"If I see cops, I'm waiting fifteen minutes."

"I get that long."

"Go to hell."

"I'm taking the rifle."

"Fifteen minutes, Jane. Then I'm getting the dog and going home."

Jimmy smoked in the truck. He face turned orange, then dark again.

"Why'd you come anyway?" Tom said.

"Fuck you."

Tom Jane walked over and got the rifle while Jimmy Ruell rolled up the window. The moonlight lit the wet hood. He handed Butts the shotgun and the kid followed and narrowed his eyes like a war-movie soldier.

They headed into the woods with the moon at their backs. The trees were small poplars and scrub oaks, and Tom and Butts sank over their boot tops in the sandy ground while their shadows slid through the weeds. They filed along the field side, where the furrows glowed in the moonlight, and Tom made sure Butts watched behind them. The creek was high and without rocks and the water came muddy and luminous and floating dead wood. Tom knelt behind a fallen hickory. The small trees bowed and the shadows twisted from the shaking branches and Butts clicked his tongue, which was their signal for danger. He shouldered the unloaded shotgun. He kicked Tom's boot and nodded at the bandolier of shells slung across his chest. Tom shook his head when he saw a squirrel silhouetted on a bare branch.

"You'd of fired," Tom said.

Butts was quiet. He looked away and chewed. Tom took the shells from his chest and gave them to Butts. "You only shoot when I shoot," he said.

The kid nodded.

"Then keep that barrel down and your finger along the trigger guard."

Butts eyed him. His nose ran.

Tom rose and waved him to his feet. They walked off in the wind, moving along beneath the stars and the wide moon. There was rain in the wind and a thin cloud cover was gathering over the bare elms that lined the river. They moved along the creek and heard the drops tapping the pooled water. The hilltop rose before them, dark against the night. The clouds mounted in layers and the moonlight went vague and the darkness was absolute in the pines that sidled along the ridge. Tom did not know what he expected walking into the trees. Perhaps taking fire and rolling for cover and shooting back at muzzle flashes in the wet dark. He waited for it, but nothing happened. He led Butts along the rowed trees, moving up and scanning the ascending ground where the pines leaned into the slope.

Tom knelt when he saw the clearing beyond the pines. There was a shack with warped boards covering the windows. He and Butts crawled toward the wood line, where the trees gave way to a makeshift pond. They rested on their elbows behind a thicket. It was half-light because of the moon and they heard nothing but the rain in the creek. Tom surveyed the garage and the road where yesterday they'd spun around in the truck. He leaned close to Butts and the kid eyed the shack.

"Break contact if there's any shooting," Tom said.

Butts put his mouth close to Tom's eye. "What's that mean?" he said.

"You fire two rounds fast and roll down the hill."

"How do you know this guy lives up here?"

"He has ideas like this."

Butts wheezed. The drizzle ran through his eyebrows.

"Jimmy's a pussy, ain't he?"

"No," Tom said. "He just grew out of things."

Toward the road, there were flooded tire ruts and a few trees. The shadows shifted when the clouds drifted before the moon. The kid buried his face in the mud and sneezed. Tom watched the black trees.

They came up the hillside and slipped in the mud and dropped their flashlights. The trees shook and a dog barked thinly. Soon two sheriff's deputies broke through the scrub, panting, and the rain blew sideways. They wore open raincoats. Tom reached over and grabbed the kid's shotgun and laid it between them. Butts started talking and Tom grabbed his mouth.

The short deputy knocked away the brown brier with his shotgun stock. Cold breath plumed from his open mouth. The flashlight beams slanted off into the darkness. The dog was leashed by a harness and it ran circles around the handler and wrapped the leash about his legs, so that the man went to his knees in the brier. The dog howled and snapped at nothing.

"Heel, goddammit," the handler said.

The dog jumped without slack. The handler was trying to free his legs and keep the shotgun out of the mud. The short deputy shined his flashlight on the handler and the wind took his hat. He laughed and said nothing and held the shotgun over his shoulder. The dog sniffed the handler's ass with a long nose and worked it like hammer.

"Need help, McGuire?"

"Go to hell."

"Now I know why you wanted that dog."

"Watch your mouth, Crick."

The dog shoved his head between McGuire's legs. He dropped the shotgun and swatted its shoulder. The dog made a game of it and snapped at his forearm.

"You just shit a T-bone?" Crick said.

McGuire belted the dog, punching the underside of its jaw. The dog whined and lifted a back leg while the handler unraveled his legs.

Butts lay there, breathing heavily. The rain pushed his bangs into his eyes. Tom kicked his boot to quiet his panting when headlamps bore across the lot and showed the rain. It was a squad car without its lights on. The engine whined and the back end fishtailed and the car slid into a small ravine where the road came up through the woods. The driver leaned on the gas, but mud sprayed from the rear tires and bent the scrub trees across the road. Soon the brake lights flickered and went dead and then a heavyset deputy crawled out in a poncho. He was illuminated by the dome light and moved slow like a man coming from a mine shaft. He stood waist-deep in water and with a hard yank pulled out a fat kid by the arm. The kid's hands were cuffed and he hit his head on the door.

The deputy pulled him out of the ditch and dragged him toward Crick and McGuire, the kid staggering behind, bound in plastic leg restraints. He wore a T-shirt and his arms were white. The deputy walked heavily in the mud and pointed with his free hand. He was shaking his head while McGuire petted the dog.

"You'll never get a wrecker up here, Bowman."

Crick nodded and held the shotgun like a suitcase. Bowman jerked the kid's arm without looking and the kid went to his knees. He vomited and panted and the dog looked at him with a tilted head.

"McGuire," he said. "Baum and the owner are in that shack. Secure it. Then look for a body."

"In this dark?" McGuire said.

"In this fucking dark."

"Where do you want the dog?"

"Just tie the shit-eater up."

Butts kept looking at Tom. His mouth hung open.

"That's the son of a bitch who had my coat," Butts said.

Tom kicked Butts in the ankle. He went quiet. They watched the handler tie the dog to the tree, where it strained against the leash and reared wildly on its hind legs. The young tree bent and sprang back and the force pulled the dog off its haunches.

The men attached the flashlights along the sides of their shotguns. The wind blew the raincoats against their legs. They walked to the shack and kicked open the door and went inside. Bowman yanked the kid and dragged him uphill. He worked his flashlight in the weeds. The kid's neck was slack and his head slumped and wagged. The beam slanted and seethed in puddles and illuminated a curled leg. He shined the light on the face of the body and then the spent shotgun shells. Tom heard the fat cop counting them slowly. Butts stared off and his legs shook from nerves.

The first deputy back through the door was bent forward. He held four sets of muddy boots and they slid from his hands. He grabbed them again, but they quickly slipped away. Tom saw the heels bounce on the gray boards. Bowman swung the shotgun against some weeds while the wind blew the raincoat tight against the deputy's stuffed backside. He looked at the boots and then at Bowman. A flashlight beam strobed across the shack's window. Bowman leaned the shotgun across his shoulder.

"Get Colonel Kurtz out here," he said.

"I can't keep a hold."

"Assess, adapt, and overcome, Crick."

The deputy looked at him and touched his face, even though his glasses were gone. He drew a troubled breath and held his side. He couldn't stand straight. The dawn broke in the east, a jagged smear of gray above the black trees. The cuffed kid lay alongside the body and screamed and made the dog turn his head sideways and howl.

"Have McGuire push from the other side," Bowman said.

"It ain't that easy."

"What's maximum effective range of an excuse?"

Crick wiped his hands on the raincoat. Bowman looked down at the cuffed kid and laughed, his mouth open.

"Zero meters ring a damned bell?" he said.

Crick turned his back to the door, bent down, and took the ankles inside his arms. He grabbed the wrists with his hands. He stood awkwardly with the rain driving against his bloated face and pulled. A leaf stuck to his bald head. His short arms didn't match the rest of him. The cold morning sun congealed behind the cloud cover and did not interrupt the darkness. The flashlight remained bright in the window and crossed and recrossed the bad glass. Tom was following it with his eyes when Butts gestured toward the shack with his head. The kid chewed on nothing and squinted his piss-hole eyes. He lay there in the pine needles with his jaw hanging.

The bodies came fast through the doorway and Crick fell backward off the porch and the mud caught him as if he were a rock. They were heaped there, wet and mired and curled like stunned salamanders. McGuire stood back in the door and shouldered the shotgun with the attached flashlight. He pointed down and chambered a round without looking away. Tom Jane saw the bearded face of his uncle in the beam. The rain nicked the mud from his belly and slanted into his balding head and his knees were drawn up to his waist. Tom thought Walt's eyes were open, but he was far away and could not tell. Butts stared hard through the drizzle while the dog wound and then unwound the leash from the tree.

Tom glanced at the gray sky, filled with rain, and at the tall trees with dead leaves hanging from the branches. The wind swept the hilltop and beat the limp pines together and then vanished. The rain fell straight down and hit the mud with violence and sound in the gray sheets of standing water. Tom looked at the blurry morning, and the dogs and the deputies became smaller, as if they had receded behind fog. The dead leaves clinging to the water black oaks were beaten away by the rain and pushed under the puddles. Soon he heard only the rain, and the scene beyond the pines swirled to dark gray. He turned and looked at Butts and the kid raised his head and strained his eyeballs. The rain gathered force and pinecones fell and then came branches of green needles. *There's no heroes, only survivors.*

"That was him, wasn't it?" Butts said.

"Come on."

"He's there. Them cops are going to do him bad."

"You see anything we can do for him?" Tom said.

He looked at Butts and then away.

"Jimmy ain't going to be there," Butts said.

"He gave us fifteen minutes."

Tom got up and started through the woods. The rain puddled the brown needles and he looked behind him for Butts to follow, but the kid was already moving. His eyes were quiet while they headed for the fields.

The sky at My Lai was white and the rains that morning settled the dust. Tom and Walt walked the grounds, carsick from the slow ride down from Da Nang along Highway 1, where old women stooped and spread rice to dry upon the broken asphalt. They'd ridden in silence, the van swarmed by motor scooters and small buses packed like elevators, with countless bicycles heaped upon the roof rack. The trip to My Lai was part of the tour. Walt had sat with sweat lines on his belly and squinted through prescription sunglasses with bifocal lenses. The van had started and stopped three times a minute for a hundred kilometers. Tom'd looked at Walt. His face had been pinched, like he was feeling this all with his kidneys.

I ain't getting out there, Walt'd said.

Just for a minute.

I know what Charlie did like they know it, Walt'd said.

Tom had said nothing.

They never tell you what those bastards did.

The driver had honked his horn and swatted flies. They'd been stuck between two buses bound for Hanoi. Arms had hung out the windows, trading dong for small watermelons from little boys who made the exchange while running barefoot. Tom's and the driver's eyes had met in the rearview mirror and the driver'd looked away. He's used to hearing it, Tom had thought. Retired officers have to be the worst.

My Lai was walled off from the rice paddies by scrub pine and evergreen. The driver stayed behind and cleaned bugs off the windshield, pouring water on the glass and scrubbing with a rag. The grounds had hand-painted signs in badly translated English, showing where a certain villager got shot. There was a bunker where a few had survived and a mosaic of an eagle's wing, powered by a jet engine, napalming women and children. The ditch was concrete and full of green water, and frogs broke the stillness for long seconds and goldfish swam with the sunlight magnifying their fins. The grass along the ditch fell under the shade of the small pines and the grass was wet in the shadows and full of lizards.

The driver had finished wiping down the headlights. He went to the back of the van and got more water. He squatted and started on the tires. Two women in dirty conical hats waited by the van with bananas and bottled water for sale. Their faces were not wrapped against the dust. They kept watch for Walt's and Tom's return and shooed away a little boy holding a mango and a broken butcher's knife. They spoke Vietnamese like hissing cats.

Tom pointed at the van.

There will be ten more by the time we go back, he said.

I can't handle the begging.

Was it like this before?

They'd fight for beer cans like they were gold.

Walt stopped before a palm tree gored by bullet holes. Incense sticks burned in bunches by all the landmarks and the smoke rose straight because the day was windless and humid. He lit a cigarette, his face red and wet. The legs of his black jeans were wrung with sweat. He put his finger inside a hole and then looked at his finger.

This never would have happened in the Marine Corps.

Why? Tom said.

Too many draftees in the army.

Didn't the Marine Corps draft then?

Walt drew on his cigarette. The incense smoke coiled.

The army got the vermin, Walt said.

Tom watched schoolchildren file into the visitors' center. The building was made of cinder blocks and had large open doors, and there were many pictures of dead children and teenage Americans smiling with rifles. The captions called the Americans mercenaries for the Saigon government. Walt had walked inside for a minute and then left to smoke. The kids wore white shirts and blue jumpers and many were screaming in the building to make an echo off the concrete. The teachers, young women in white ao dais, *put fingers to their small mouths. They tried talking about the pictures, pointing and narrating slowly. The children yelled louder and laughed at their echo.*

Walt studied the pole where the Vietnamese flag hung limp. The white-winged egrets left fast moving shadows upon the ground and they impaled his own shadow. The white light seared Tom's neck, the backs of his ears. He rubbed on sunblock, but his skin was sweaty and the cream proved useless. Walt looked at the ditch and dry grass that sprouted through the concrete sides, and it was a creek now and not a ditch at all.

We protected them the best we could from Charlie, he said. I used to give this one little boy rides on my bulldozer. He'd bring his sisters. Even the dogs stayed close to us marines. The people knew.

They never followed the army? Tom said.

The draftees were scum. They didn't care who they shot.

Walt pointed at the ditch. The cigarette burned between his fingers.

Marines would have never done this, he said.

Tom felt like the sun was pushing him into the sandy ground. My Lai is so small, he thought. He didn't know where the people would have had room to die.

Walt looked over at the kids and smiled. They played a game with sticks and a ball in the shade of the building's awning.

You got any of that candy? Walt said.

Tom nodded and took a Ziploc bag of suckers from his knapsack. Walt walked down the footpath with the candy. The mortar between the stones was crumbling and the stones were loose. Walt grinned. He gave the kids a thumbs-up and the peace sign. They saw him and rose like a wave and screamed and ran for the wall. Their ball rolled down the small walk and out into the sun. They cowered along the wall and pressed their faces to the painted cinder blocks. Kids looking out the windows disappeared. Walt held the candy and they screamed louder. A little girl was bleary-eyed, her face wet, as if melting. She tried climbing inside through the window, jumping up and looking behind her. One boy ran screaming, his arms outstretched like airplane wings. The teacher came outside and ignored Walt and ordered the children into the building. She pointed the way. Her hand were small and very beautiful, and Tom watched his uncle stare at her soft fingers and shake the bag so the suckers knocked together. He stood there even after the kids had filed inside to see the pictures of the dead.

20

Jerry Bowman leaned back on the chair after he and Walt lit cigarettes off the same match. His stomach untucked his shirt. The cell had been recently painted and the brush hairs were dried into the cinder-block walls. Walt sat on the edge of his bunk. He held the cigarette between his teeth while he rolled up the wide cuffs of his orange jumpsuit. His stomach already poked against the worn canvas from ten days in the Hall County Jail, eating trays of breaded veal patties and chili mac and chicken-fried cube steak with mashed potatoes and corn. There were more sheriff's deputies than inmates—just Walt and a goofy kid named Anders, who'd drawn two months for stealing Christmas lights off the houses in town—and the food was for the deputies. The kid was in the cell opposite, but he slept all the time, and his nose had gotten broken during the arrest. Walt had plea-bargained for six months' county time on some complicity charge he didn't understand and agreed to testify at all three trials. Bowman slowly rocked on the back chair legs and exhaled the smoke in thin streams.

"You was up on the DMZ the whole time?" Bowman said.

"We staged out of Dong Ha. You was army?"

Bowman nodded and looked at his hand. "Americal division. South of Da Nang. A war of land mines for me. I maybe saw VC three times in a year."

"I saw plenty of regulars. I was at Con Thien."

"Battalion size?"

"In the A Shau."

"Calley was in the other battalion."

"No shit."

"I understand what made those guys do it."

The fluorescent lights streaked the waxed floor tiles and Walt heard voices down the hall.

"I went back there. This last spring."

"You said that."

"There's a palm tree with bullet holes at My Lai."

"Fuck them. They were laying the mines."

Walt leaned forward and rested his elbows upon his knees. Bowman lit another cigarette off the one he was finishing.

"They still use the roads you jarheads built?"

"And the bridges. Ferry launches. All of it."

"We were there for nothing and they made out."

"I don't know."

"Shit, Bud Roe, I wasn't asking you a question."

Walt stared unblinking at him. He still had bandages around his wrists. Bowman tapped the cigarette with his middle finger and exhaled the smoke sideways.

"It's big with Baum. They're holding him in Rock Island County. Even if the murder charge don't stick, he's looking at forty years. They're trying those kids as adults."

"I'll tell what I know."

"Federal people are looking into it."

Walt didn't answer. He rose from the cot and stood by the painted bars. Then he sat back down and leaned against the cinder blocks. Bowman looked at his fingernails and pushed the cuticles down with his cigarette lighter.

"You might be testifying for a while on this one," he said.

"I did what I did."

"You're all right, jarhead. Next week, I'll ask about making you a trustee. What'd you do down in Watega?"

"I was a professional Vietnam veteran."

"Shit."

"Ask anybody," he said.

"You never wore jungle fatigues and marched in a parade?"

Walt lit another cigarette.

"Why you ask?"

"Because I hate those assholes."

They sat quietly and listened to the heat pour inside through the vents. The cell was without windows, and Walt stared at the cinder blocks, imagining one that looked upon a river, high from spring rains, coursing through forests of hardwoods where the branches curled over the water. He was sitting against a tree, watching the eddy swirl and twist and foam, when a voice sounded from down the corridor.

"Hey, Sergeant. Visitor for Walt."

The guys called him by name. They liked him that way.

Bowman's knees popped when he stood and opened the cell door. Walt stepped into the hallway. Bowman left the door open.

"We make you a trustee," he said, "we don't got to close this at night."

Walt nodded and Bowman held the key ring.

"We'll make that kid do the cleaning. Me and you will just bullshit. I can take you out in the truck and everything. I know a few places."

They walked down the short hallway and Bowman opened one more door.

"You ice fish?" he said.

"Sure."

"I can even take you deer hunting. I'm retiring next summer. I really don't give a rat's ass what they say."

"Short-timer," Walt said.

"So short, I could dangle my feet from a dime. You know. Play handball against the curb."

The old man was looking hard at Walt when Bowman walked him into the dayroom. The rain blew against the three barred windows. On the ledge were two Coke cans used for spittoons. The old man sat on a plastic chair and held a brown paper bag. He shook his head and drank coffee from a Styrofoam cup and set the bag on the table. Walt watched his pleated throat swallow and then looked out the window, where the old man was reflected very small. The room was hot and he had not taken off his coat. Bowman shook the key ring while the rain splattered the glass, and many times the old man's image melted and re-formed.

"Take your time, jarhead," Bowman said. "Coffee's on the county."

He slapped Walt's back and left the room. The keys jangled down the hallway. The old man's stare was fixed and Walt looked away at the coffeemaker beside the pop machine, where a handwritten sign warned TOUGH SHIT ON REFUNDS. There were no cups left. The glass pot was stained brown and powdered creamer dusted the brown floor tiles. Walt listened to the rain and the compressor from the pop machine. The old man gave a wet cough, then fell into a long fit and beat the table when his swallowing did not stop it. His eyes turned wet and red.

"You tell your vet buddy what you pissed away?" he said.

Walt turned while the old man wiped a coat sleeve across his lips. He hacked again. Acid refluxed from his throat. He spat into the coffee cup.

"Hell no," he said. "You just cried and *semper fi*'d."

"He was army," Walt said.

"So you just welcomed each other home."

Walt said nothing.

"God, those kids beat the hell out of you."

The old man set the bag on the table. He took folded papers from his coat and laid them flat. The rain stopped but not the wind, and it blew the water from the glass in twisting lines.

"I brought you some socks," he said. "Now sit down and sign these. She's divorcing you. I paid her off. The house is mine."

Walt nodded and sat down.

"She's thirty grand richer," the old man said. "That comes out of your inheritance."

"Tommy bring you?"

"I drove myself. He says he saw you being drug out in handcuffs."

"Yeah."

"He brought home this crazy kid. He works, but he's plain-ass goofy."

Walt looked at the papers. The old man drew *X*'s where he needed to sign and Walt did.

"What the hell were you thinking?"

"I wanted away."

"You're the one who marries them. I pay for the divorce."

"Why do you pay?"

"Because the bill comes to my house."

The old man looked at the papers. He ground his teeth together.

"You a dammed doctor?" he said. "Sign so people can read your name. And when you come home, be ready to work."

Walt capped the pen. Outside, the rain blew from the trees and spun in the gray light. The old man folded the papers and stood. His forehead was wet from the hot room.

"You got to call a guard to leave?" he said.

Walt nodded and studied the rain and thought of dancing to rock and roll music in a room all alone.

"I don't know," he said.

21

The Department of Corrections bus left Joliet while the dry snow whirled across the cornfields and drifted along the snow fence. Dwight leaned his cheek against the metal grate covering the windows. The cold seeped through the glass and made his eyes water and bleared the inmates wearing khaki uniforms and surplus peacoats. The bus was half-empty and smelled of pine disinfectant and cold sweat. Many sat dozing chin to chest and their heads bounced when the tires hit potholes. Some talked in low tones and chewed gum with open mouths. The youngest men looked around the bus with wide eyes and they wore their watch caps high upon their heads, so the material slacked and stuck straight. The guard was a heavyset Mexican and he sat behind the cage door by the driver, scratching his mustache with his thumb. A pump shotgun rattled in the rack by the door. His eye whites were hangover red. The inmates looked up at him; they looked away; they looked at their shoes.

The little black sat in the seat opposite Dwight and was singing soulful tunes. He cupped his hand and put it over his mouth and crooned into that. His head swayed; his eyes floated; he rocked back and forth. Dwight could see that he wanted to let go. The guard rapped on the cage with his knuckles and the black looked up into his bloodshot eyes. He quit singing. After awhile, Dwight fell into talking with him. He had a gold tooth.

"You got to get a good job inside," the black said. "That's essential."

"You've been to prison?" Dwight said.

"No."

Dwight nodded and glanced outside. Frank Sinatra sang on a casino billboard while the snow slammed into his face. He looked around the bus, careful not to make eye contact. The men were either skinny or fat and most had wet coughs. The guard yawned and fought to keep his eyes open. This was not at all what Dwight had thought it would be like.

"I bet being a janitor is the best job for me," the black said. "I can walk around singing all day. I'll have two years to get my shit right."

"Sure."

"There won't be no singing if I get in the kitchen. Too many guys in there. One of them will jack me over it."

"Why's that?"

"They won't like songs from back in the day."

Dwight didn't know what he was talking about.

"You just got two years?" he said.

"Four. But four is two. You get a day for a day."

Dwight waited for the black to ask him about his sentence. He never did.

"I got twelve and a half, then," Dwight said.

The black closed his eyes and sang without volume and the cold breath plumed from his nose. The guard looked at the black where he swayed and mouthed words. He'd been massaging his red eyes. He chewed gum with an open mouth and seemed dizzy and looked away, shaking his head. He said something to the driver and belched into his cupped hand.

Dwight looked through the wire grates when a Camaro was passing the bus. It was primer gray and the body putty above the wheel wells was sanded smooth. The driver honked while the snow disappeared into the windshield. A few men looked out, and for a long second the car stayed beside the bus. The windows were smoggy from a bad defroster and Dwight could not see who was honking. He hoped a woman was driving the car and that she was unbuttoning her shirt to give the men one last look. Maybe even lifting her skirt and spreading her legs to touch herself.

22

Tom Jane and Butts walked in Ho Chi Minh City and wiped the sweat from their faces, and their hands came away filthy. They drank water fast and it drooled from the corners of their mouths. Out in the street, the motor scooters squalled from roundabouts like sideways rain and the exhaust whirled in the white light and made cyclo drivers hack phlegmy gouts while they peddled three rotations before coasting through the shadows of the plane trees. The cyclos hauled caged ducklings, fifty-pound rice bags, raw pork quarters stained the light color of the dust.

"Shit if I ain't wrung-out," Butts said.

He looked at the dust impacted in his palm lines and then at the sidewalk stalls selling the same Ho Chi Minh T-shirts and bootlegged 'N Sync CDs from Hong Kong, and the deadpan Vietnamese vendors all looked back and squatted on lean haunches.

"You'd think at least one of them would try selling something different," he said.

Tom Jane closed his eyes among the horn blasts and the

babies crying from rice baskets and the clubfooted shoe-shine boys who limped like three-legged dogs.

They're here someplace, even if Walt says they're fat old men working in lawn mower factories. I bet I can still see them walking in their jungle fatigues with a twenty-four-hour pass not fifteen minutes old while the neon bar signs blink and seethe upon these sidewalks wet from the rain that quit only a second ago. I'll meet them and they'll know me and we'll drink Tiger beer and shots of Johnnie Walker Red and hoot and holler like carny barkers while the bar girls swing naked from poles and a slicked-back dink sings Elvis songs into a karaoke machine but doesn't know enough English to find the piss can.

Butts hit Tom's shoulder and he opened his eyes. A one-eyed Vietnamese squatted upon his thin haunches and held a hand-rolled cigarette between his middle fingers. He pointed to his wares: T-shirts and baseball hats with the Communist star and knockoff Teva sandals. Butts chewed tobacco and he couldn't make his mouth wet enough to spit.

"Back in the war," Butts said, "this is one of the places where them shoe-shine kids would blow up an American."

"What do you know about back in the war?"

"Goddamned History Channel. Me and your grandpa was watching it. I bet some of these guys sold Americans snow cones full of glass. Even shit worse than that."

Tom watched two cyclo drivers passing them. One was missing an arm below the elbow; the other had blue eyes and looked Italian. They smiled with black saw teeth, almost having a contest over who could nod the fastest. Their conical hats were marbled with sweat and grease.

"They got to sell some different shit around here," Butts said. "Maybe some lemon shake-ups and them elephant ears with powdered sugar. They could have some games set up where you win goldfish. Like them BB machine guns."

The Vietnamese was scratching under his grubby eye patch when Tom saw the old Zippos for sale. The lighters had Mickey Mouse with eagle wings spitting fire from the sky; others showed Mickey giving the world the finger, and one had Mickey doing Minnie doggy-style, *DEROS to Dreamland 8-1-71.* Then Butts cackled like crows over garbage. The kid shook a fat bottle of rice wine and the cobra inside knocked against the glass. The amber wine canted the white sunlight. Butts turned the bottle upside down and the snake's tongue fell slantwise from its mouth. He giggled and stuck out his own tongue and the Vietnamese laughed the smoke from his mouth.

"This here's a real-life cobra," Butts said. He spoke like he was telling Tom something he didn't know. "I bet the toughest Mexican wouldn't eat this."

"That's not tequila."

"I bet back in the war the Mexicans thought it was. They probably ain't got worms over here anyway."

"Put it down," Tom said. The kid's shaking had uncoiled the snake.

"I bet they even drank it with lemons and salt."

Butts shook faster and made bubbles. The cobra turned upside down and the tail lodged into the bottle neck. Sweat ran off Butts's skinny elbows, and Tom imagined the bottle flying up a second before it did. Butts flailed his arms and grabbed after it like a fumbled ball and came back with handfuls of air. The bottle bounced once before shattering. The amber wine soaked Ho Chi Minh's pinched face on the T-Shirts and then leaked many lines into the shallow gutter and muddied the dust. The cobra flopped on the Zippos, nearly white from the alcohol, before a kid with dirty knees snatched it and ran off between a barber and his haircut customer, who was slouched in a street-side chair.

The Vietnamese smoked his cigarette and looked at Tom. Butts stared at the broken glass. Tom handed the Vietnamese a one-hundred-dollar bill and the man nodded briefly and his good eye bulged. He grinned, toothless. He jumped off his rickety haunches and went headlong into the scooter traffic, and the other vendors fought over his wine-soaked wares. They threw elbows. They hissed like snakes. Conical hats flew off heads. A little shoe-shine boy crawled between Butts's legs and jumped before him, then laughed with his tongue aloll and shook his shoe-shine box. He tried handing it off to Butts. An old woman stuck out her tongue and did the same thing with a basket of taro roots. She could walk, but not well.

"Shit," Butts said. "What they want?"

"You break, I pay."

The shoe-shine boy grabbed at Butts's sneakers. A little girl with matted hair jumped in front of him. She sold bottled water from a bucket heavy with ice and it pulled her to one side. The boy was on his knees, already working the brush, his eyes focused like a gem cutter's. The girl shoved a water bottle in his hand. Butts tried walking away but gave up. Men in worn khaki looked up from steaming bowls of noodle soup. They sat on plastic stools, laughing and waving their chopsticks.

"They'd of killed you right here," Butts said.

"You think so?" Tom said.

"I bet some son of a bitch died where I'm standing."

Tom looked where the man's wares had been. Only the broken glass remained. The Zippos were the first things taken. *I might even be one of them, fresh in from the Iron Triangle or Tay*

Ninh, and on a staff sergeant's pay, I'd have money for two boom-boom girls.

Butts threw a handful of dong bills on the sidewalk. He ran to the curb when the kids scattered and fell upon Ho Chi Minh's blue face. Two cyclos made their way past young girls on bicycles, the panels of their white *ao dais* wrapped around their waists. The old woman with the taro roots was screaming. Two cyclos hauled yapping puppies in birdcages. They crawled over one another and shoved their noses against the rusted wire. An old man with a mangled cheek came from the shade of a sagging awning to see. Butts tilted his head and spat. He looked at Tom and spat again, his mouth never closing right.

"They must be bringing them dogs to a pet store," he said.

"No," Tom said. "To the butcher."

"Piss on that."

The old man with the eye patch looked at Butts and grinned. His teeth were tar black. "Dog and snake wine make you strong," he said. He cackled and pointed up the street. He yelled over his shoulder in Vietnamese and the men eating soup howled and barked. Butts eyed them all like a movie cowboy.

"Son of a bitch, no," he said.

Tom grabbed his shoulder.

"Come on," he said.

"Come on hell."

Butts took off running after the last cyclo while the men screamed and fell sideways from laughter. Tom went after him. A lone cop in yellow khaki blew a whistle and pointed into the street with a varnishless nightstick. The motor scooters came like squalls, weaving between cyclos and women carrying sacks of mangoes, and the wind blew the yellow leaves from the plane trees. Tom watched Butts grow small in the traffic. He was running hell-bent after those dogs, his fists already clenched.